Ever After High™

Next Top Villain

Have you read these titles
from Ever After High?

The Storybook of Legends
Shannon Hale

The Unfairest of Them All
Shannon Hale

A Wonderlandiful World
Shannon Hale

Once Upon a Time
Shannon Hale

Digital short stories

The Tale of Two Sisters
Shannon Hale

Duchess Swan and the Next Top Bird
Suzanne Selfors

Lizzie Hearts and the Hedgehog's Hexcellent Adventure
Suzanne Selfors

Ever After High™

EVER AFTER Royals!

Next Top

Villain

EVER AFTER Rebels

A SCHOOL STORY

Suzanne Selfors

LB

LITTLE, BROWN BOOKS FOR YOUNG READERS
www.lbkids.co.uk

For Isabelle and Walker

LITTLE, BROWN BOOKS FOR YOUNG READERS

First published in the United States in 2015 by
Little, Brown and Company
First published in Great Britain in 2015 by
Little, Brown Books for Young Readers

3 5 7 9 10 8 6 4

A CIP catalogue record for this book
is available from the British Library.

ISBN 978-0-349-12459-9

Printed and bound by CPI Group (UK) Ltd, Croydon, CR0 4YY

Papers used by LBYR are from well-managed forests
and other responsible sources.

MIX
Paper from
responsible sources
FSC
www.fsc.org FSC® C104740

Little, Brown Books for Young Readers,
an imprint of Hachette Children's Group
and published by Hodder and Stoughton Limited
338 Euston Road, London NW1 3BH

An Hachette UK Company
www.hachette.co.uk

www.lbkids.co.uk

Contents

$\mathcal{D}$ear reader,

Look for this throughout this book.

When you see it, you'll know it's a point in the story where you can rewrite someone's destiny with the companion hextbook: *General Villainy: A Destiny Do-Over Diary*! Inside that diary are lots of activities inspired by the events of this story. Grab a copy so you can flip the script!

XO
The Narrator

Swan

Song

To be born a fairytale princess is a blessing indeed, but hers is not the lazy, carefree life that many imagine. There are numerous, important decisions that a princess must make every day.

For example, how would she like to be awoken in the morning? Should she choose an enchanted alarm clock to sing and dance around her bedroom? Perhaps her parents could employ fairies to gently sprinkle waking dust on her cheeks. Maybe she'd

prefer to have a household troll ring a gong or her MirrorPhone blare the latest hit song.

Duchess Swan, a fairytale princess proud and true, chose none of those options. Instead, she liked to be awoken by her favorite sound in the whole world.

Honk! Honk!

"Don't tell me it's morning already," a voice grumbled.

Duchess opened her eyes. While the honking had come from the large nest next to her bed, the complaining had come from across the room. To her constant dismay, Duchess did not sleep alone. This was the girls' dormitory at a very special school called Ever After High, and her roommate was Lizzie Hearts, daughter of the famously angry Queen of Hearts. Lizzie was not a *morning* person. Which is why she didn't own an alarm clock.

Honk! Honk!

"For the love of Wonderland!" Lizzie exclaimed, her voice partially muffled by a pillow. "Off with the duck's head!"

Duck? Duchess frowned. *Seriously?*

"Pirouette is *not* a duck," Duchess said, sitting up in bed. "Pirouette is a trumpeter swan."

"Duck, swan, pigeon...she's *loud.*" Lizzie burrowed beneath a jumble of blankets.

"Of course she's loud," Duchess said. "She's named after a trumpet, not a flute."

Honk! Honk!

Duchess waved, to let Pirouette know that she hadn't gone unnoticed. Then Duchess pushed back the lavender silk comforter and set her bare feet on the stone floor. It was the first day of the new school chapter, and she was looking forward to her new classes. Why? Because each class was another opportunity to get a perfect grade. As a member of the Royals, Duchess took her princess duties very seriously. One of those duties was to be the best student she could be.

But there was another truth, somewhat darker and simmering below her perfect surface. Duchess Swan was well aware that grades were something she could control, while her ill-fated destiny was not.

Tendrils of warm air wafted from the furnace vent, curling around her like a hug. She pointed her toes, then flexed, stretching the muscles. It was important to keep her feet limber, for she was a ballerina, and her feet were her instruments.

Honk! Honk!

"Okay. Hold your feathers." Duchess slid into her robe, then opened the window. A gust of fresh morning air blew across her face. Pirouette flew outside, heading for the lush green meadow. A swan needs to stretch, too.

Just as Duchess tied the laces on her dress, the bedroom door flew open and two princesses barged in. "Ever heard of a little thing called *knocking?*" Duchess asked.

"Can we talk?" the first princess said. Her name was Ashlynn Ella, daughter of the famously humble Cinderella. She yawned super-wide. "It's about your alarm clock."

The second princess, whose name was Apple White, daughter of the famously beautiful Snow White, also yawned. "Yes. Your goose alarm clock."

"She's not a goose," Duchess sighed. These princesses really knew how to get under her wings. "She's a swan."

"Oh, that's right. Sorry," Apple said.

The two princesses, having just rolled out of bed, looked unbelievably perfect. No bedhead, no sheet lines, no crusty sandman sand at the corners of their eyes. Apple was known as the Fairest One of All, and Ashlynn couldn't be any lovelier, even if she tried.

"Apple and I agree, as do the other princesses, that the honking sound that comes from your room every morning is starting to become a bit of a royal pain."

Royal pain? Duchess looked away for a brief moment so they wouldn't see the twinge of hurt feelings.

"I'd be happy to lend you some of my songbirds,"

Ashlynn said. Then she whistled. Three tiny birds flew through the doorway and landed on her outstretched finger. "It's such a cheerful way to wake up."

"Bird alarms aren't always reliable," Apple said. "I'd be happy to connect you to my network of dwarves. They'll send a wake-up call to your MirrorPhone."

"I don't need your songbirds or dwarves," Duchess told them, a bit annoyed.

Okay, she was more than a *bit* annoyed. Those girls were always acting as if they were better. They really ruffled her feathers!

Ashlynn, Apple, and Lizzie were of royal heritage—the blood daughters of fairytale kings and queens. Being a Royal at Ever After High meant being part of the most popular and the most privileged group. Duchess was also a Royal, but she was different. Most Royals were destined to marry other Royals and rule kingdoms, living out their lives in comfort, health, and fortune. In other words, a big, fat Happily Ever After was waiting for most of them.

But Duchess did not have such a future, nor did she have a future as a dancer. Her destiny, as the daughter of the Swan Queen, was to turn into a swan and live out her days web-footed and feathered.

You can't perform a graceful *grand jeté* with webbed feet!

To make matters worse, she had no Happily Ever After with a charming prince written into her story.

Although Duchess's future did not seem fair, she'd accepted her circumstances. It was her duty to keep her story alive by fulfilling her destiny. She worked hard at her studies and her dancing. She did her best to make her family proud. But it drove her crazy that these girls had nothing more to worry about than being awoken by honking. It was just as Duchess often said: Birds of a feather flock together.

Lizzie popped her head out of the covers and glared at the intruders. "I order this meeting to be over. Now!"

"Sounds good to me," Duchess said. "Even though

I was so enjoying our little chat." She forced a smile. "However, it's time to get dressed for class. And you know what happens if you're late." She looked directly at Ashlynn.

"Oh my godmother, thanks for the reminder," Ashlynn said, her eyes widening with worry. If she was even just one second late, her clothes would turn into rags. She picked up the hem of her nightgown and rushed out the door, her songbirds following.

"Well, I'd better go, too. I hear my magic mirror calling. Charm you later," Apple said.

Duchess's smile collapsed the moment the princesses were gone. "Good riddance," she muttered under her breath.

"If my mother were here, she'd order their heads chopped off," Lizzie said. Then she burrowed back under the blankets.

Just as Duchess closed the bedroom door, Pirouette flew back in through the window. She landed at Duchess's feet, then turned the corners of her beak

into a smile. Duchess knelt and gave her a hug. The wonderful scent of wind clung to Pirouette's white feathers. "Lucky girl," Duchess whispered. "You don't have to deal with know-it-all princesses."

Duchess filled a bowl with swan kibble—a mixture of breadcrumbs and grains—and set it on the floor. Pirouette began eating her breakfast. This was the calmest time of the day for Duchess, before the flurry of classes and activities, while Lizzie snored peacefully. And Duchess usually began each day by writing in her journal.

She sat at her desk and opened the top drawer. There was no need to hide the golden book, because it was enchanted with a security spell. She pressed her fingers against the cover. A click sounded. This was the only place where she shared her truest of feelings—her darkest of secrets. After turning to a blank page, she dipped her quill into ink and began to write. But one thought filled her mind. One thought that never seemed to go away. And so she wrote:

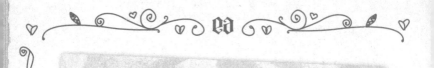

I wish I had a Happily Ever After like Ashlynn's and Apple's.

Then Duchess Swan looked out the window and sighed. Being a perfect princess meant she had to accept her destiny, even if that destiny was covered in feathers.

$\mathcal{D}$uchess learned about her destiny on the morning after her eighth birthday, when she awoke and discovered that her feet had changed overnight.

It was a terrifying sight. "Grandma!" she cried. "What happened?"

Her grandmother pulled back the covers, took a peek, then sat calmly at the edge of the bed. "Dear child," she said. "This is the beginning."

"The beginning of what?" Duchess asked. She pulled her knees to her chest so she could get a

closer look. Her feet, which had been normal when she'd gone to sleep, were now flat, black, and webbed. "Take them off," she said, pulling on them as if they were shoes. "Make them go away!"

"They will go away," her grandmother said. "Don't worry. You will learn how to make them come and go as you please."

But they didn't go away. They stayed while she got dressed and they stayed while she ate breakfast. She tried to squeeze them into shoes, but they wouldn't fit. "I'm not going to school like this!" Duchess insisted.

"A princess must be educated," her grandmother said, gently pushing her out the palace door. "A princess must never be ashamed of who she is."

The village kids pointed and laughed as Duchess waddled down the lane, her big, flat feet making flapping sounds. "She looks like a duck," they said. "Ugly duck, ugly duck."

She felt ugly.

The webbed feet disappeared later that day. After

school, Duchess ran home, barefoot, and didn't complain about the sharp rocks in the lane. She was so happy to have toes again!

More changes came that year. She grew taller, her legs turning as skinny and gangly as a bird's. Sometimes when she laughed, she'd honk, which made all the other kids laugh. In the mornings, she'd find white feathers in her bed.

And she began to crave the plants that grew in the pond behind the schoolhouse. Spring green and tender, they looked so delectable. One day she waded in and began to eat them. "Look! The princess has flipped her crown. She's eating weeds!" Luckily, the village children didn't notice her also eating the little water bugs that skimmed the pond's surface. They tasted just as good as the cook's roasted beast.

What is happening to me?

Then, one morning, while walking home from school, Duchess spied a downy feather floating in the wind. It looked exactly like the feathers she often found in her bed. She chased after it, then saw another, and another, drifting in the distance. The trail led her to the lake behind the palace, where a bevy of swans had gathered. Although they migrated to the palace grounds every winter, Duchess had never paid close attention to them. She knew that they were beautiful, with their snowy white feathers, black beaks, and black eyes. But as she sat in the grass, watching them preen and glide, she came to an amazing realization. Their swan feet looked exactly like the webbed feet she'd grown.

She was one of them!

And so, Duchess began to teach herself how to control the changes. It was not easy, for a sneeze could turn one arm into a wing, or a laughing fit could make a beak appear. By the time she was ten, she could control the transformation. She could turn herself into a swan whenever she wanted.

She saved this reveal for a special day at spellementary school. It was late spring and the class

was lined up along the edge of the swimming pool. "Today we will learn how to do a swan dive," her teacher, Mrs. Watersprite, said, pointing to the highest board. The students lined up at the bottom of the ladder. There were many trembling legs and terrified squeals as they climbed. "This is the most graceful dive of all," Mrs. Watersprite explained. "Put your hands above your head, lean forward, and jump! Then spread your arms wide, like wings."

One by one, the students jumped. Some clawed at the air as if trying to stop the fall. Some landed on their bellies. Others went feet first. "No, no, no!" Mrs. Watersprite hollered. "That was not graceful!"

Duchess went last. She raised her arms above her head and gripped the end of the board with her toes. It was a long way down. The other students looked small, some shivering beneath their towels. With their faces turned upward, they waited for the ugly duck girl to jump.

"Dive!" Mrs. Watersprite ordered.

Duchess bounced three times, then jumped. Just as gravity grabbed hold of her, she reached out her arms, closed her eyes, and transformed.

The dive was perfection. When she rose to the surface, the village kids cheered.

And that day, the ugly duck girl became the swan princess.

*S*oon after all the various alarm clocks had chimed, buzzed, tweeted, and chirped, the class lists for the new chapter were delivered. A fairy-godmother-in-training *poofed* into the room and dropped two envelopes onto Duchess's desk and one envelope onto Lizzie's.

Duchess was dressed and waiting. As usual, she'd laid out her clothes the night before. She'd neatly packed her bag with her tutu, tights, and pointe shoes. She'd already brushed her long hair, which

hung in lavender, white, and black stripes. And she'd selected her favorite headpiece—a strand of pearls that looped around her head and was secured by a single, perfect white feather.

As the fairy-godmother-in-training disappeared in a cloud of pink smoke, a flurry of activity arose on the other side of the dorm room. Lizzie Hearts was running late, as usual. Mornings were always a major drama. "Why didn't anyone lay out my clothes? Why do I have to choose what to wear? Has anyone seen my scepter?"

"If you took the time to be organized the night before, then you wouldn't have to go through this every morning," Duchess said.

"The word *organized* doesn't even exist in Wonderland," Lizzie said. "Besides, if I were back in Wonderland, I'd have my own playing-card army to help me in the morning. I'm still not used to doing all these chores by myself." She pulled a comb out of her black hair. "Oooh, I've been looking for this."

Duchess hurried over to her desk and picked up the first scroll. A swan symbol had been pressed into the wax seal.

Dearest Duchess,

I hope this letter finds you well. Each time I look out the window toward the pond and see the swans, I think of you. Without your companionship, the days feel long, but I know that you are doing your duty, and that is more important than my boredom.

We are so proud that you continue to get perfect grades at Ever After High, just as your mother before you. You bring honor to our family.

Your loving grandmother

Although Duchess missed her home and her family, there was no time for homesickness at that moment. There was another envelope to open, and it contained the list of new classes. After breaking Headmaster Grimm's wax seal, she unfolded the parchment. Everything looked to be in order: Advanced Ballet at the Red Shoes Studio, Princessology with Mrs. Her Majesty the White Queen, Home Economyths with Professor Momma Bear, Damsel-In-Distressing, and—she gasped.

"What the hex? Why am I registered for General Villainy with Mr. Badwolf?"

Pirouette, who was sitting in her nest, looked up from her preening and shrugged her wings. The nest was made from rushes that had grown in Duchess's backyard.

"This must be a mistake." Duchess reread the list. "I'm not supposed to be in that class."

"We have a saying in Wonderland," Lizzie said. She sat on her closet floor, tossing things over her head as she put her outfit together. A heart-shaped purse

whizzed past Duchess and hit the wall. "If you're not *supposed to be*, you should not *be supposing*."

Duchess frowned. That sort of nonsensical thing came out of Lizzie's mouth all the time. It was called Riddlish, and only those from Wonderland seemed to understand it.

Why'd we get assigned as roommates? Duchess wondered for the umpteenth time. Over the chapter break, she'd filled out the roommate selection form. She'd even submitted an essay, describing her perfect match as someone who is tidy and organized, and likes birds. The word *messy* had not appeared anywhere in her essay. No matter how many times the cleaning fairies visited, Lizzie's side of the room always returned to disaster status.

It was a mystery why they'd been assigned to the same room. Just as it was a mystery why Duchess had been placed in General Villainy.

"Aren't you going to read your scroll?" Duchess asked.

"I will, as soon as I find my deck of cards." Lizzie

crawled under the bed, then reemerged with the deck in hand. While Duchess possessed the magical power of transformation, Lizzie's power was to build anything with her deck of Wonderland cards. This came in handy if an extra chair was needed, or a ladder, or an umbrella.

Lizzie opened her envelope and read out loud. "Princessology. That will be super-easy. I already know all that stuff. Anger Magicment. Why do I have to keep taking that class? I'm trying to control my temper, not lose it. It makes me so angry that everyone expects me to be angry!" She stomped her foot, then kept reading. "Drama. Ooh, that will be fun. Maybe I'll get the lead role this year. And General Villainy. Ick, that sounds dreadful. And it's the first class. Talk about starting the day on the wrong side of the card deck. But at least we have it together."

It made sense that Lizzie would be selected for General Villainy. Her mother was a notorious queen whose temperamental outbursts were legendary.

But why me? Duchess thought. *Have I done something wrong?*

Suddenly, Lizzie dove into a pile of socks. "There you are," she said, pulling out a round, prickly lump. "You silly little thing. I've been looking for you for days." The lump uncurled, then wiggled her nose. Her name was Shuffle, and she was Lizzie's pet hedgehog. "It's time to go to class," Lizzie told her. Then she tucked the critter into her book bag.

The hallway filled with the sounds of footsteps and chatter as girls headed out of the dormitory to their first classes of the day. Duchess left the window open so Pirouette could come and go as she pleased. Then she and Lizzie joined the stream of students.

Despite the fact that they were opposites in many ways, Duchess was glad to have Lizzie by her side as they negotiated the crowded hallways of Ever After High. Lizzie might lack organizational skills, but she certainly didn't lack confidence. "Out of the way!" she ordered, waving her scepter as if she'd already been crowned.

They passed through the Common Room, ducking beneath the tree branches that grew inside the school. They grabbed brioches and orange juice from a Castleteria cart. All the students were talking about their class lists.

"Why are you walking so fast?" Lizzie complained.

"I want to get there early so I can tell Mr. Badwolf to transfer me to another class," Duchess informed her.

Lizzie swung her bag over her shoulder. "Can you do that? Headmaster Grimm makes all the class decisions. There must be some reason why he included you." She took a bite of breakfast.

"Putting me in General Villainy doesn't make sense," Duchess said, her brow furrowing beneath the pearl strand.

Lizzie swallowed. "We have a saying in Wonderland: *The rhythm of time brings the telling of rhyme.*"

"What's that supposed to mean?"

"It means all answers will be revealed in time."

That was a nice thought, but the truth was, Duchess didn't have time on her side. She had only these moments at Ever After High to do her best, to get perfect grades, and to live her life before her destiny caught up with her.

They finished their breakfast. Then, just as they left their juice containers with the recycling fairy, Lizzie cried, "Oh no!" Her hedgehog had leaped from the book bag and was running as fast as her pudgy little legs could carry her, which wasn't very fast. Because the courtyard was so crowded, the critter managed to disappear in the maze of feet. "Bad hedgehog!" Lizzie called. Then, in much the same way that Duchess transformed from a person into a swan, Lizzie transformed from a girl who'd been happily eating a brioche to an ill-tempered future ruler. "I hereby order someone to stop that hedgehog!" she hollered, waving her scepter. "Watch your feet or heads will roll!"

"Looking for this?" a voice asked.

Shuffle had curled into a ball and was lying in a pair of cupped hands.

Strong hands.

Duchess's gaze traveled up a letterman's jacket and rested on the most handsome face she'd ever seen.

Her heart began to pirouette.

A Charming Crush

Duchess had learned, as had most everyone at Ever After High, to never look directly at Prince Daring Charming's mouth when he smiled. How he got his teeth to glow so blindingly white was a Charming family secret. The shine was powerful enough to melt chocolate hearts.

And *real* hearts.

"You naughty hedgehog." Lizzie plucked Shuffle from Daring's hands and plopped her back into her book bag.

Daring puffed out his chest. "No need to thank me. Rescuing fair damsels is what I do."

"I don't *need* to be rescued," Lizzie informed him. "I'm perfectly capable of catching my own hedgehog." She squared her shoulders in a proper way, but Duchess could tell, from the softening expression on Lizzie's face, that she was grateful. She just couldn't admit it in public.

Duchess pushed a strand of lavender hair from her eyes and gazed up at the face that was only an arm's length away. *Daring Charming.* His name sounded like muse-ic. An entire chapter in her diary was dedicated to him. She thought he was one hundred percent perfect. Among the royal princes at Ever After High, Daring was the most handsome, the most swoon-worthy, the most amazing example of princeliness the world had ever seen. And she'd been smitten with him since . . . *forever after.*

"Both our names begin with the letter *D*," she said dreamily. Daring and Lizzie turned to stare at her. *Oops.* She hadn't meant to say that out loud.

A chorus of giggles arose from the edge of the courtyard, where Daring's groupies had gathered to catch a morning glimpse of their favorite prince. They took pictures with their Mirror-Phones. Adoration clung to Daring like paint to a wall. Was every single girl at school in love with him?

"Well, gotta go. Riddle you later," Lizzie told him as she started walking again. Duchess followed. She couldn't get away fast enough. *Both our names begin with the letter* D. How embarrassing.

"Uh, hold on, Lizzie." Daring darted in front of the girls, blocking their path. As he smiled, they both shielded their eyes. "I was wondering if you'd like to do something with me, but then I asked myself, why waste time wondering? Of course you'd like to do something with me. Who wouldn't?" He winked. The groupies sighed in unison.

"Do something?" Lizzie asked. "You mean like..." She smiled sweetly. "Chop off your head?"

That was funny. Duchess tried to stifle her laugh

by holding a hand over her mouth, but the *honk* escaped through her fingers.

Daring glanced at her. "Did you just *honk?*"

"Uh-huh." Duchess's cheeks began to heat up.

He looked at her as if he'd never seen her before. "You look slightly familiar."

"I'm Duchess," she said with a little wave. "Duchess Swan." She'd introduced herself at least a dozen times already. They'd even had a class together.

"I'm sure you're enchanted to make my acquaintance," he said. Then he turned his attention back to Lizzie. "So…" He leaned closer. He didn't seem to notice that Lizzie was scowling at him. "We could go for an evening stroll. My face looks stellar in moonlight. But come to think of it, I look great in sunlight, too. Candlelight, lamplight, firelight—you really can't make me look bad." He ran a hand over his blond locks.

Am I hearing things? Did he just ask her out? Duchess checked her ears, to make sure there weren't any feathers stuck in them. *What about*

me? She imagined Daring dancing a *pas de deux*, standing at her side, lifting her into the air with his strong arms. Twirling around and around on the dance floor.

Lizzie's hedgehog had once again escaped the book bag and was climbing up Lizzie's arm. "I don't want to take a stroll with you," Lizzie said. "I get plenty of exercise on the Croquet Team."

Duchess's mouth fell open. Lizzie turned him down? Was she *mad*?

Shouts arose from the groupies. "I'll go on a stroll."

"Take me strolling."

"No, take me!"

Daring scratched his head in wonderment. "Did you say you *don't* want to go? With me?"

"That's what I said," Lizzie confirmed. She pried Shuffle off her arm and tucked her back into the bag.

"But . . ." Daring looked about as confused as the Emperor had when he discovered he wasn't wearing clothes. "Is that possible?"

"Possible is as possible does," Lizzie said in a very matter-of-fact manner.

Duchess Swan was no expert on love, but she assumed, by the way Daring was gazing at Lizzie and by the way Lizzie kept looking past his shoulder as if she had someplace more exciting to go, that the crush was one-sided.

Just like Duchess's crush.

"I'll go on a stroll with you," Duchess wanted to say, but the five-minute warning bell chimed. She snapped out of her daze, remembering that she needed to talk to Mr. Badwolf. "Come on," she told Lizzie. The two girls sidestepped Daring, then hurried across the cobblestones.

"Out of the way!" Lizzie hollered at the groupies, who hastily scattered. "I hate getting angry so early in the morning," she told Duchess. "I don't know how my mother does it. She has at least fifty temper tantrums a day. I've only had a few, and I'm already exhausted."

Lizzie didn't seem one bit happy that she'd been

asked on a date by the royal hunk himself. How was that possible?

Duchess wiped a crumb from the corner of her mouth. But the lingering sweetness of the brioche had become tainted by the bitterness of envy.

ver After High did not look like your typical campus. Perched on a bluff, the school itself was a hodgepodge of halls, rooms, and towers that rose high above the Village of Book End. Some of the towers were so tall that they pierced through the clouds. All the balconies provided breathtaking views of the surrounding forests, farmlands, and meadows. Trees were welcome to grow inside, and so they became part of the structure, supporting ceilings with their branches and cementing the foundation with their roots. It was a living building of sorts, filled to the brim with energy and magic. And stairs.

Lots and lots of stairs.

Duchess and Lizzie stood at the end of a hallway, in front of a narrow door with a sign that read, TO THE DUNGEON.

"Ugh," Lizzie said. "I hate dungeons."

"Me too," Duchess said. The dungeon back home had a few ancient skeletons and smelled like rotten eggs. She'd gone down there once, on a dare from the cook's boy. She never went again.

It made perfect sense that a class specializing in villainy would be held in a dreary place. At least she wouldn't have to spend more than a few minutes down there. She'd get Mr. Badwolf's permission to transfer and be on her way.

The stone stairs were steep and slippery. "Did I miss the hext about wearing hiking boots?" Lizzie grumbled as she clung to the wrought iron railing. Her red heels were not designed for this sort of terrain. Duchess's shoes weren't much better, but she wasn't going to take them off and risk stepping on a spider, or something worse.

Just above their heads, stone hands stuck out of the wall. Each hand held a lighted torch. The flames cast strange shadows. Cobwebs sparkled between the stones. Something darted in front of them. "Was that a rat?" Duchess cried.

"A *rat*...*a rat*...*a rat*," echoed down the stairs.

"A rat the size of a cat," Lizzie said. Shuffle squealed and burrowed deeper into Lizzie's bag. "Oh my wand, there's another one. Professor Piper needs to clean this place up."

They reached the bottom of the stairwell, only to find another set of stairs, this one even narrower and steeper than the last. Lizzie groaned. "You'd think that Headmaster Grimm could at least put an elevator in this place. Seriously. Don't the villains deserve better?"

There was some truth to that. Villains were just as welcome at Ever After High as the heroes. Both

had equally important roles to play in fairytales. Without darkness, there couldn't be light.

"An elevator would be nice," Duchess said as she brushed a cobweb from her nose. She couldn't wait to be in the fresh air again. Neither her ballet side nor her swan side wanted to be underground. Dancers jump; birds fly. Dancers leap; birds soar. They do not tunnel!

Another sign waited at the bottom of the second stairwell.

THIS WAY TO DUNGEON, COACH CLASS
THIS WAY TO DUNGEON, FIRST CLASS
THIS WAY TO THE CREEPY CELLAR
THIS WAY TO THE CAULDRON ROOM

"Cauldron room," Duchess said, pointing. With Lizzie still in the lead, they hurried down the dimly lit corridor. Dampness glistened on the stone walls. Pairs of small red eyes glowed from the ceiling. The girls doubled their pace.

The door to the cauldron room had been propped open by an empty cauldron.

"It's hot in here," Lizzie complained as they stepped inside.

The feather on Duchess's headpiece immediately wilted. It was like stepping into a sauna. The source of the heat was a fire burning in a large stone hearth. Three cauldrons were suspended over the flames. The first bubbled with thick green swamp water. The second popped and sizzled with blood-red lava. The third swirled like a whirlpool of mud.

Lizzie and Duchess both peeled off their jackets.

"It's much cooler over here," a girl called. Her name was Ginger Breadhouse. She was sitting on a wooden stool, as were three other students. The remaining two stools were empty.

The bell rang. Lizzie hurried across the stone floor and grabbed one of the stools. She set her book bag on the floor, then waved for Duchess to join her. But Duchess decided to stand by the door and wait for the teacher. No reason to get comfortable if she wasn't staying.

A deep clearing of a throat startled Duchess. Mr. Badwolf entered the room, a clipboard in his hands. He was immaculately dressed in a three-piece plaid suit, a pocket kerchief, and a bright red necktie. His gray hair hung in thick, luxurious waves. He sniffed the air, then looked at Duchess with his yellow canine eyes. Her heart fluttered for a moment. Wolves are hunters. If she turned into a swan at that very moment, would he pounce on her?

But no pouncing occurred. Nor did he ask Duchess why she was standing alone by the door and not sitting with the others. He adjusted his tie, then strode across the room. "Welcome, future villains," he said, his voice deep and growly. "I am your instructor, Mr. Badwolf."

"Excuse me," Duchess said as she followed him. "But there's been a mistake." She held out her letter. "I'm listed in this class, but I'm not supposed to be here. My name is Duchess Swan."

"Yes, I know who you are," he said, his pupils narrowing.

"Oh, great. Well, then I'd like your permission to transfer to another class. Something more fitting."

"More fitting?" He raised his bushy eyebrows. "Are you not good enough for this class, Ms. Swan?"

One of the students giggled.

Duchess squared her shoulders. "Of course I'm *good enough*. I'm good enough to do anything," she said proudly. "But I'm not evil. I mean, there's no evil in my bloodline. So I don't think I should be in a villain class."

"Is that what you *think*?" He took the parchment from her and wrote in big red letters: TRANSFER DENIED. Then he handed the parchment back.

"But…"

Mr. Badwolf growled. It wasn't a ferocious, loud growl—rather it was soft, as if given as a warning. "Sit down, Ms. Swan."

Duchess gasped. Then, with angry footsteps, she marched over to the last stool and sat with a loud *hmph*.

Lizzie whispered, "Bet you're feeling a little bit evil now."

She was. She wanted to give Mr. Badwolf a piece of her mind. She wanted to tell him that not only was she *good enough* for this class, but also that she was *better* than this class and everyone in it!

Mr. Badwolf stood with his feet wide apart, holding the clipboard behind his back. "Does anyone else have any *personal issues* they'd like to bring to my attention?" He was clearly being sarcastic, but Lizzie's hand shot up anyway.

"Yes, I have a whole list of issues. I would like this class to begin later. It's soooo early and I need extra time in the morning to find everything because my playing-card army is back in Wonderland. I also think we need to have an elevator installed. I cannot be expected to hike up those stairs every day in my heels. And the rats are scaring my hedgehog. I'd like you to do something about that." She folded her hands in her lap, waiting for his response.

The big wall clock *tick-tock*ed. The cauldrons

bubbled. But none of the students said anything. They sat, waiting to see what Mr. Badwolf would do. Duchess figured that if he helped Lizzie with some of her requests, then surely he'd reconsider Duchess's request for a transfer.

He narrowed his eyes and glared at Lizzie. "If you are worried about rats, Ms. Hearts, then I suggest you and your hedgehog each get a rabies shot. I get mine every year." He jangled a tag that hung on a chain around his neck.

The only boy in the class laughed. His name was Sparrow Hood. Lizzie shot him a nasty look. Then she said, "I have no intention of getting a rabies shot. I got all my shots back in Wonderland. I've been vaccinated for walrus warts, teapox, and March Hare madness."

Mr. Badwolf ignored her. He removed his pocket kerchief and brushed dust from the edge of his desk. Then he sat. "General Villainy is one of the most demanding classes at Ever After High. If you manage to get an A grade, you will join the ranks of students before you such as the Wicked Stepmother, the Billy

Goats Gruff Troll, and myself, of course." He smiled, revealing a row of sharp canine teeth.

An A was the highest grade in each class. Duchess had a perfect score of A's on her transcript.

Mr. Badwolf continued. "Each of you has been hand-selected by the headmaster himself to attend this class because each of you has the honor of being the son or daughter of a confirmed villain or being closely related to someone evil."

Duchess's hand shot up. "Um, excuse me, but—"

His eyes flashed. "Interruptions are not allowed in my classroom," he snarled.

Her hand fell to her side. *What a grouch.*

"As I was saying, each of you is here because you come from an evil bloodline. *Or*"—he looked at Duchess—"you have the capacity to be the first in your family to go bad."

Go bad?

A chill ran up Duchess's spine.

Rebel

Roll Call

While the cauldrons provided a background melody of crackling and popping, Mr. Badwolf tapped his finger on the clipboard. His fingers were furry and his nails were long and black. They looked like claws. He seriously needed a mani-curse at the Tower Hair Salon. "Roll call. First up, Faybelle Thorn."

The girl sitting next to Duchess slid off her stool. "Here," she said in a serious way. Duchess didn't know this girl. In fact, she'd never seen her before.

She was dressed in midnight-blue leggings and a shimmering tunic. "I am sooooooo happy to be here. I've been waiting for this class my entire life." As she smiled at Mr. Badwolf, a pair of little iridescent wings unfurled from her back.

Duchess frowned. The girl was a fairy, but not the small kind who worked throughout the school and lived in the Enchanted Forest. Human-sized fairies could be notoriously wicked.

"I admire your exuberance, Ms. Thorn, but an overflowing exhibition of happiness is not evil."

Faybelle stopped smiling.

"You have been selected for this class, Ms. Thorn, because your mother is the Dark Fairy, who cursed Sleeping Beauty. Would you like to tell the class a little about yourself?"

"You bet." Faybelle pulled a pair of pom-poms from her book bag, then cartwheeled to the front of the class. "Faybelle, Faybelle, she's the one! She's the one who'll make evil fun!" Each time she jumped, her little wings beat the air. "Give me an *E*. Give me a *V*. Give me an *I*. Give me an *L*. What does that spell?"

No one answered.

Faybelle floated a foot off the ground. "Come on, team! Where's your Ever After spirit? What does that spell?"

"It spells *evil*," Duchess said.

Faybelle blinked her fairy eyes. Then she flew over to Duchess and floated in front of her. "I wasn't asking you, because *you* don't belong in General Villainy class."

Duchess shrugged. Despite the fact that she was being snooty about it, Faybelle *was* making her point for her.

"Your snarkiness is appreciated, Ms. Thorn," Mr. Badwolf said as he wrote on his clipboard. "Hextra credit for you."

Faybelle smirked at Duchess, then returned to her stool. But not before aiming fairy dust right up Duchess's nose. Duchess sneezed, but it came out as a honk.

Mr. Badwolf ran his finger down the clipboard. "Next up is Ginger Breadhouse."

"Here." Ginger stood and waved to everyone. Her pink hair was tied into ponytails, and all the embellishments on her dress made her look like a decorated cookie.

"Ginger has been selected for this class because her mother is the Candy Witch, who tried to eat Hansel and Gretel. Would you like to tell the class a little about yourself?"

Everyone already knew Ginger. She did a Mirror-Cast show called *Spells Kitchen*, during which she made fabulous desserts. Ginger walked to the front of the class, a box tied with yellow ribbon in her hands. "I just want you to know that even though my mom tried to eat some kids, I would never do that." Her eyes twinkled behind her pink glasses. "I love to cook, but *none* of my recipes call for boys or girls." She tugged on the yellow ribbon, then opened the box. The scent of pure deliciousness filled the air. Sweet and cinnamon spicy, it was a

welcome relief from the weird cauldron odors. "I baked these for everyone. They are miniature cinnamon trolls." She handed one to Mr. Badwolf. White icing dripped off the troll-shaped pastry.

He wolfed it down in one bite, then smacked his lips. "Even though it contains no raw meat, it was delicious," he reported. Ginger smiled proudly. "However, delicious is not evil." Mr. Badwolf wrote on the clipboard. "I am very disappointed in you, Ms. Breadhouse. Next time you bring treats for the class, I suggest that they be poisonous. You get a DG for the first day."

"What's a DG?" Duchess asked. They didn't have that grade in other classes.

"DG stands for 'do-gooder,'" Mr. Badwolf said. "DG is the worst grade you can get in General Villainy. Some would argue that it is even worse than a fairy-fail grade." He grabbed another troll.

With a confused look on her face, Ginger returned to her stool.

"Next up we have Lizzie Hearts," Mr. Badwolf said.

"Here!" Lizzie had been feeding Shuffle a piece of cinnamon troll.

"Ms. Hearts was chosen because she is the daughter of the notorious Queen of Hearts. I have great hexpectations for her, but I have heard a rumor that she's been trying to control her temper. Is this true, Ms. Hearts?"

"Yes," Lizzie replied. Mr. Badwolf raised his bushy eyebrows. "I mean, *no!*" She jumped from her stool. "I would never try to control my temper. Someone is spreading fables and that makes me feel very, very *angry!*" She kicked over her stool. Her face turned as red as her shoes.

It was a brilliant tantrum, but Duchess knew the truth. Lizzie wanted to be an angry queen as much as Duchess wanted to be a permanent swan.

"Most hexcellent," Mr. Badwolf said as he wrote on the clipboard.

Lizzie grabbed the stool, uprighted it, and sat back

down. As she dabbed sweat from her upper lip, she gave Duchess a questioning look. She'd played her role, but what would Duchess do?

"Next up is Sparrow Hood."

Sparrow sat slouched on his stool, a guitar leaning against his leg. He was dressed in mossy, forest colors. His studded vest matched his studded boots. His chestnut hair hung over his eyes, which were closed.

"Sparrow?" Lizzie nudged him. He bolted upright.

"Dude, I was trying to sleep."

Mr. Badwolf tapped his long nails on the desk. "Mr. Hood, villains do not sleep. Villains disrupt the sleep of others. Keep that in mind."

Sparrow yawned, then scratched his soul patch. "Haven't you heard of chillin' like a villain? I was up all night practicing my riffs." Sparrow was the lead singer and guitarist in a band called the Merry Men.

Mr. Badwolf growled. "Your *riffs* will not earn you an A in this class, Mr. Hood."

"Total bummer. Well, maybe I don't want to earn

an A," Sparrow said with a shrug. "Why am I here, anyway? My old man wasn't evil."

"You are here because your father, Robin Hood, was a notorious thief. Thievery is an excellent trait in a villain. And there are times when you appear to have the appropriate attitude," Mr. Badwolf said. "But because your father used his thievery for good, there was great debate among the faculty whether you should be in this class. You have much to prove, Mr. Hood."

"Proving stuff sounds like way too much work," Sparrow said. "My guitar and I have better things to do." Then he lowered his hat so the brim shaded his eyes. Was he going to nod off again?

Duchess squirmed. This class seemed a waste of time. And the roll call had been a total disaster. So far, only one student actually wanted to be a villain. Sparrow didn't even care what grade he got. How could he not care about something as important as that?

"Our next student needs no introduction," Mr.

Badwolf said. He looked straight at a girl who sat in the corner, hidden in the shadows. The room went silent. Even the cauldrons stopped bubbling. The girl slowly stood, then stepped into the light. She was tall and imposing, with ebony hair that cascaded down her back. Her purple skirt matched the purple highlights in her hair and was covered in a filigree lacework. Her eyes were as dark as a raven's—hence, her name.

"Hi," she said with a frown. "Well, I'm sure we all know why I'm in this class."

Raven Queen was the daughter of the infamous sorceress the Evil Queen, who'd tormented royals from one kingdom to the next, including Snow White. Raven's mother was so evil that she went beyond her own story and invaded Wonderland, infecting its madness. And that was the reason why Lizzie hadn't been home in a very long time.

But Raven Queen had recently become noto-rious for something that had nothing to do with her mother. Raven was the leader of the Rebels, a

growing group of students at Ever After High who dared to question their destinies. This had been the case ever since Legacy Day, when Raven had refused to sign the Storybook of Legends.

It was normal to ask questions about the future. Duchess asked plenty of questions, but she did this privately, in her diary. To be a Royal meant to have pride in one's heritage and to take one's role seriously. The Rebels didn't seem to care about tradition. They chose to act in ways that went against their destinies—but if they didn't live out their destinies, their stories might disappear forever after, which affected everyone. Raven had refused to sign her name in the Storybook of Legends on Legacy Day. This had never happened before. *Never.* And now all kinds of characters thought they could be free to live whatever life they pleased. Raven was to blame. She was selfish, in Duchess's opinion.

"Raven shouldn't be in this class," Faybelle said loudly. She'd taken the words right out of Duchess's

mouth. "She's doesn't have the right to be a villain anymore."

Raven didn't defend herself. She stood with her shoulders slouched, as if she carried the burden of her family legacy on her back. "I guess there's no use in asking for a transfer."

"If she gets a transfer, then I should get one, too," Duchess said.

"There will be no transfers," Mr. Badwolf barked. "Despite Ms. Queen's recent decision to lead a rebellious uprising—"

"Hey, I'm not *leading an uprising*," Raven insisted. "I'm not telling other people what to do. If they choose to question their destinies, then that's their decision."

Duchess sneered again. Maybe Raven wasn't giving speeches about rebelling, but she was leading by example. And actions were more powerful than words.

The fur on the back of Mr. Badwolf's neck bristled. "Don't huff and puff at me," he told Raven.

"The facts are indisputable. You carry more evil in your bloodline than the rest of the students combined. The faculty and the headmaster are hopeful that you will change your mind and embrace your destiny." He pointed to a large wooden sign that hung on the wall.

THOU SHALL NOT STRAY FROM THY STORY.

After a long, heavy sigh, Raven slid back into the shadows.

Mr. Badwolf picked up the clipboard and read. "The last student on the list is Duchess Swan."

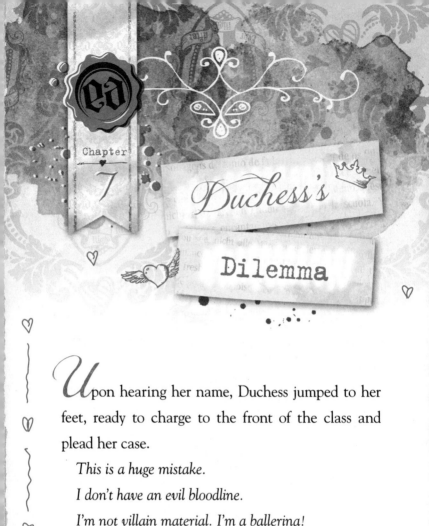

Duchess's Dilemma

*U*pon hearing her name, Duchess jumped to her feet, ready to charge to the front of the class and plead her case.

This is a huge mistake.

I don't have an evil bloodline.

I'm not villain material. I'm a ballerina!

But Mr. Badwolf did not invite her to introduce herself. Nor did he offer an explanation as to why she was there. "Sit down, Ms. Swan," he said.

What the hex? Everyone else got the opportunity to speak. "But—"

A low growl rumbled in Mr. Badwolf's throat. His eyes flashed. Duchess sat. The morning was not going as she'd planned. And one student had already earned hextra credit. She had nothing but frustration and questions.

Mr. Badwolf proceeded to hand each student a thick hextbook, *A Guide to General Villainy*. Then he wheeled a chalkboard to the front of the class and, with a piece of white chalk, began to draw. The students watched in silence, except for Sparrow, who'd started snoring. Lizzie prodded him with her scepter. He woke up and yawned.

"Can anyone tell me what this is?" Mr. Badwolf asked as he pointed to the board. He'd drawn a triangle. Inside the triangle was a stick figure with a curly tail.

No one answered. Faybelle shrugged. Ginger licked frosting from her fingers. Duchess fumed.

"This is a pig," Mr. Badwolf explained. "And this is its newly built straw house."

"Good thing you're not teaching Arts and Crafts," Sparrow said with a snicker.

"I like your drawing, Mr. Badwolf," Faybelle said. "It looks exactly like a pig." She waved her pompoms. "Give me a *P*. Give me—"

"Not now, Ms. Thorn." Mr. Badwolf pressed his long, furry fingertips together. "The question I pose to you, students, the future creators of chaos, is this: What would you do if you wanted to eat this little pig but it was hiding in its house made of straw?" Faybelle's hand shot up. "Yes, Ms. Thorn?"

"I would order takeout," she said with a smile.

Mr. Badwolf scowled at her. "That is not the correct answer." He turned to the next student. "Ginger, I pose the question to you. If you wanted to eat the pig, how would you get it to come out of its house?"

"I don't eat pigs," Ginger said. "I know a few, and they're very nice."

"Incorrect," Mr. Badwolf snarled. "Mr. Hood?"

"Dude, it doesn't matter to me," Sparrow said with another yawn. "Get the pig, don't get the pig. I really don't care. Unless you want me to write a song about it."

A little white cloud burst from Mr. Badwolf's hand as he crushed the piece of chalk. "That. Is. *Incorrect!*" His upper lip rose, exposing his sharp teeth. "Ms. Hearts? Surely you know the answer!"

Wheezy, deep breathing was coming from Lizzie's book bag. Her hedgehog had eaten so much cinnamon troll she'd fallen into a sugar stupor. "I'd knock on the door and ask to come in," Lizzie said with a smile.

Mr. Badwolf growled in a most displeasing way. Lizzie grabbed her scepter and jumped to her feet. "I meant to say that I'd pound on the door, real hard, and yell as loud as I could, 'In the name of the queen, I command you to come out of that house or you shall lose your piggy head!'" Then she sat back down. "But I wouldn't really chop off its head. I agree with Ginger. Pigs are nice."

Mr. Badwolf looked as if he might explode. If he'd been a teapot, steam would have shot out of his ears. "That is the worst answer I've ever heard!" He stomped both of his feet, which were rather large. The chalkboard trembled.

"Wow," Lizzie whispered to Duchess. "He's better at temper tantrums than I am."

Mr. Badwolf whipped around and faced Duchess. "Ms. Swan, what is *your* answer?"

Duchess didn't care that Mr. Badwolf was practically foaming at the mouth. He'd had his rabies shot, after all. What she cared about was getting transferred from this class. "I don't think I should answer that question. I'm not a villain, and—"

"Wrong, wrong, *wrong*!" Mr. Badwolf ended the sentence with a howl.

Duchess sighed. This was a total waste of time. She could be practicing her arabesque at the dance studio, or writing her deepest thoughts in her diary.

Mr. Badwolf smoothed his hair and took a long,

deep breath, composing himself. Then, his voice steady and calm, he looked toward the dark corner. "Surely *you* know the answer, Ms. Queen?"

Raven fidgeted on her stool. She sighed, then hung her head. "The answer you're looking for is to huff and puff and blow the house down."

"Yes," Mr. Badwolf said with much relief. "Yes, indeed. Finally, a correct response."

Duchess was immediately alarmed. Was Raven trying to get a good grade in this class? Maybe the *best* grade in the class?

Duchess's hand shot up. "I've changed my mind. I'd like to answer the question." She slid off her stool. As she smoothed her white embroidered skirt, her thoughts spun like a dancer who'd lost control. *What do I say? What's better than huffing and puffing?* She cleared her throat. "I would...I would..." Her legs went a little weak as she realized she had no answer. Mr. Badwolf stared at her, waiting.

Raven broke the silence. "I've also changed my mind," she said. "The pig worked hard building his

house. Hard work should be rewarded, not destroyed. I would let him live in peace."

Mr. Badwolf sank onto the edge of his desk, his head shaking with frustration. "You are the worst group of future evildoers in the history of this school. You will all bring shame to yourselves, to your families, and to fairytales everywhere."

Shame to my family? Duchess practically wilted.

"I hope it is not too late to save you from your goodness," Mr. Badwolf said. He walked over to the chalkboard, grabbed a new piece of chalk, and wrote:

Thronework assignment:

Do something rotten and nasty by the end of the school day Friday.

"Yay!" Faybelle cheered as she rustled her pom-poms. Everyone else groaned.

"The one student who does the rottenest and nastiest thing by the end of school Friday will get an A for the week. The rest of you will get an FF."

FF stood for "fairy-fail." "To make it more exciting, the student who earns the A will have the opportunity to pick a prize from my own personal treasure vault." He crossed the room, and, after whispering a secret password, a section of the stone wall slid open. Gold and silver light filled the cauldron room.

Suddenly interested in the proceedings, Sparrow Hood leaped from his stool and ran to look inside the vault, his fingers twitching as he gazed upon the piles of gems and jewels.

"Is that a silver muffin pan?" Ginger asked.

Faybelle pointed to a golden megaphone. "I'd love to cheer with that."

Lizzie liked the heart-shaped pendant, while a golden quill caught Duchess's eye. "Look at all that loot," Sparrow said. "One of those golden arrows could buy some sound equipment and a new set of drums for the band."

Mr. Badwolf plunged his hand into a chest of gold coins. "Practice your thieving skills, Mr. Sparrow, and one day you will possess your own treasure vault."

Raven was the only student still sitting on a stool. "I don't care about treasure," she said.

"Of course she doesn't," Faybelle whispered to Lizzie. "Her mother's the richest woman in the world."

Having overheard Faybelle's comment, Duchess narrowed her eyes. Raven Queen did seem to have everything, and all she did was complain about it.

The school bell rang, indicating that class was over. The students grabbed their book bags. Sparrow grabbed his guitar.

"Look to your family stories for inspiration," Mr. Badwolf called as the students headed for the exit. "And remember, only one of you can earn an A for the week."

Failure was not an option for Duchess Swan. If she couldn't get transferred, then she'd have to do her best. And her best meant perfection.

Guess I'll be doing something rotten and nasty.

A Scoop

of Snoop

The Castleteria was bustling with activity as students ate lunch. Hagatha, the lunch lady, was an expert at fixing meals for all sorts of palates and all sizes of stomachs. Porridge was always on the menu, as were curds and whey. The day's lunch special was cheeseburgers, grilled by dragon fire, with a helping of enormous green beans, provided by the giants. Duchess really liked green things, so her plate was piled high.

She sat at her regular table. Sometimes Lizzie ate

with her, but sometimes Lizzie joined the other students from Wonderland. Duchess had tried sitting with them, but the constant stream of Riddlish had made her head hurt. She'd tried sitting with the other Royal princesses, but the conversation always turned to the tension between the Royals and the Rebels, which ruined her appetite. Those Rebels were always creating drama when it wasn't needed. They should be focused on their grades and doing their best, like she did.

Duchess didn't mind eating alone, especially on that particular day. She had a lot to think about. She picked up a giant green bean and began to gnaw on it the way one gnaws on an ear of corn. What rotten and nasty thing could she do by Friday? How could she compete with students whose blood contained the DNA for evil?

"Hello, fellow fairytales," a voice called. The mirrors mounted on the Castleteria walls suddenly lit up. "It's time for a brand-new edition of *Just Right!*" Theme music for the popular MirrorCast began to play. Everyone stopped eating, or walking, or talking, or all of the above, and turned to watch the nearest mirror. A face appeared—a very smiley, very perky, very pretty face that belonged to Blondie Lockes, the host of the show.

Blondie, the daughter of Goldilocks, told everyone that she was a Royal, though this was in doubt. She called herself a reporter, but in Duchess's opinion, that was also in doubt. Blondie was a snoop, and no information was safe around her.

"As usual, I have the latest scoop on what's happening at Ever After High," she announced with a smile.

Even Duchess set down her green bean. Blondie might have been as annoying as a feather tickling one's nose, but who doesn't love the latest gossip? What was Blondie going to spill today? A secret romance? A broken curfew? Another student deciding to become a Rebel?

Blondie's mane of thick curls bounced against her shoulders. "On this very morning, Raven Queen and five other students in the General Villainy class were named the worst group of future evildoers in the history of our school by Mr. Badwolf. And that is a direct quote from the spider who sat beside her."

Murmurs arose in the Castleteria. Duchess looked across the room to the corner table where Raven was sitting. She was watching a mirror, just like everyone else.

"But Raven and the others have a chance to make things just right." Blondie pressed her face so close to the camera you could count her freckles. "Each student in General Villainy must commit a rotten and nasty act by the end of school on Friday or fairy-fail the assignment. She or he who commits the most rotten and nasty act by the end of school on Friday will get an A and the chance to pick a prize from Mr. Badwolf's treasure vault." Blondie adjusted the bow that sat on top of her head. "The student who wins will be on the right path to evil success. Will it be Raven? Will it be Sparrow or Lizzie? The question of the week is: Who will be the Next Top Villain?"

The words NEXT TOP VILLAIN filled the mirror.

"It's gonna be me!" The camera shot widened. Faybelle stood beside Blondie and looked right into the camera. "Raven Queen doesn't want to be a villain, and the rest of the students are all do-gooders. I'm gonna win for sure. Faybelle, Faybelle, she's the one. She's the one who'll make evil fun!" She did a couple of super-high kicks.

Blondie stepped in front of the bouncing cheer-hexer. "You heard it here first. Faybelle Thorn claims she's going to be Ever After High's Next Top Villain. I'll see you soon with the latest scoop. Remember, if it's not too hot or too cold, it must be *Just Right!*" The mirror returned to normal. Raven Queen went back to eating her cheeseburger. And everyone else went back to living their fairytale lives.

"What are we going to do?" Lizzie asked as she slid next to Duchess onto the bench. Her lunch tray held a pot of tea and a plate of little heart-shaped sandwiches. She dropped four sugar cubes into her teacup. "I don't want to do something rotten and nasty."

"Me neither," Duchess said.

"But there's so much pressure to live up to my mother's reputation." Lizzie sighed. "You're so lucky you don't have to worry about what other people think."

"Lucky?" Duchess pushed the green beans aside. "I'm also feeling the pressure. My family insists that I get perfect grades."

"Hexpectations, schmexpectations!" Lizzie said as she stirred her tea. "As we say in Wonderland, out of the moat and into the boat."

"What does that mean?"

"It means we're in the same boat," Lizzie said. "The same predicament. How are we going to pass this class when neither of us is a villain at heart?" Then she looked up and groaned. "Oh no, here he comes."

Daring Charming strode across the Castleteria on a direct course for their table, his groupies close behind. Duchess grabbed a napkin and wiped her mouth. Then she fussed with her hair and her pearls.

Was he still looking for someone to take that stroll with him?

"Ladies," he said, striking a manly pose. "I'm sure you're charmed to see me again."

"Hello, Daring," Lizzie said, sounding about as prickly as a hedgehog. She took a bite from one of her sandwiches. "What do you want now?"

"I'm getting my hair trimmed this afternoon. I give the clippings to my favorite charity, BGGB. Blond Guys Gone Bald." He smiled, and Lizzie's silver teapot illuminated. "I usually get a good turnout audience-wise, so I wanted you to know that I'm happy to save a seat for you. You might get a few bits of hair in your eyes, but that's a small price to pay for a front-row view."

"I'll go," Duchess said.

Daring ignored her. He stared expectantly at Lizzie. "I'm awaiting your reply."

Hello? Did she blend into the wallpaper? *I'm right here.*

"I'm way too busy," Lizzie said. "I've got serious thronework to do."

"Then, as the perfect hero, I offer my assistance to the damsel-in-distress." With a flourish of his brawny arm, he bowed. *How romantic!* Duchess's heart did a little tap dance behind her rib cage. "I shall assist you, Ms. Lizzie Hearts, with your thronework."

But rather than accept an offer of help from the most handsome prince on campus, Lizzie Hearts rolled her eyes. "It's not for Damsel-In-Distressing class, Daring. Besides, you can't help. You don't know anything about being a villain."

"Well, that's true. I excel at all things goodly and courageous. But perhaps we could—"

"I gotta go," Lizzie said as she scrambled to her feet. "See you later, Duchess." Then she grabbed her tray and hurried away. Daring stared after her, his perfect face clenched in a puzzled expression. Clearly, he wasn't used to being turned down.

"I've got the same thronework," Duchess told him hopefully. Would he bow and offer to help?

But before she could explain further, Prince Daring Charming was already walking away.

"Totally awkward." Sparrow Hood slid onto the bench and grabbed one of her green beans. "How can you eat this stuff? I mean, don't get me wrong—I like the color green. But these things are so stringy I could make music with them." Then he pretended to play the bean. "Hey, do you know you've got a little something stuck between your front teeth?"

Duchess's hand flew to her mouth, and she picked out a green bean string. *Great.* She'd smiled right at Daring. This day just kept getting better and better. "What do you want, Sparrow?"

"Chill, Swan. I just wanted to talk to you about something." He glanced over his shoulder, then lowered his voice. "I think we should team up."

"Team up? And do what?"

"And live happily forever after."

She froze. Those three words made her stomach clench. "You know that's not my destiny."

He pushed his hat off his brow and grinned.

"Relax, I'm just messing with you. Actually, I was thinking we could team up and win this villain thing."

"And why would I do that?"

"Because we're both outsiders." He leaned his elbows on the table, and his voice took on a conspiratorial tone. "Look, the rest of them—Ginger, Lizzie, Raven, and Faybelle—they've got evil in their blood. But as far as I know, you don't have a drop and neither do I. And to make things worse, my dad was a do-gooder. The odds are against us, Swan. But if we team up, we might just ace it."

"You don't care about grades," Duchess said. "Besides, Mr. Badwolf said that only one student will get the A." She narrowed her eyes. "I know what you're doing. All you care about is your music. Everyone knows you hate thronework. You're trying to trick me into doing all the work for you."

He put a hand on his chest. "Oh, Swan, you're breaking my heart. How can you say such things? Don't you know there's something else I care about?

Something other than my songs?" He leaned close and gazed into her eyes.

Duchess took a sharp breath. Was this his way of telling her that he liked her? "I don't know what you're talking about," she said coolly.

"My dad's motto was 'Rob from the rich and give to the poor.'" He jangled a golden wristband. "But my motto is 'Rob from everyone and give to me.'" He swung his legs around and stood. "You can have the grade, but I want to pick the prize from Mr. Badwolf's treasure vault." Then he slung his guitar over his shoulder. "So, whadda ya say? Are we going to do a duet?"

She frowned. Sharing a thronework assignment with the one guy in school who was known for his laziness was the last thing she wanted to do. But he had a point. Without a drop of evil in their blood, how could they compete?

"I'll think about it," she said.

uchess's afternoon class was Advanced Ballet, taught at the Red Shoes Studio, which was a short walk from the main campus. With her book bag slung over her shoulder, she hurried down the lane. She was tempted to transform into her swan self and fly there, but thanks to the addition of the *General Villainy* hextbook, her bag was much too heavy to carry in her beak.

Only a few students at Ever After High knew the joy of flight. Those with fairy wings and flight-casting

abilities could zip betwcen classes if they chose to. But a fairy possesses a human shape, which is not streamlined like a bird's. Duchess knew how to point her neck and beak, creating a line that cut through fierce wind. She knew how to catch updrafts between her feathers and how to float as if she were made of cloud.

She could re-create those sensations on the dance floor, soaring on two legs as if she were dancing on air.

Duchess opened the oak door and stepped into the Red Shoes Studio. A grand ballroom spread before her. Hundreds of pairs of dancing shoes hung from the high ceiling. In the corner, a shoemaker stood at the very top of a wobbly ladder, hanging another pair. The soles of each shoe had been worn out. The twelve Madames who taught at this school were the same twelve princesses who'd left their palace each night to secretly dance until dawn. And each night, they had danced so much that they wore out their shoes. Though older now, the Madames still loved to dance, and that was why they employed a troupe of shoemakers, whose little hammers and sewing machines could be heard from the back room as they constantly made new shoes.

Duchess slipped into a dressing room and changed into her leotard, tights, and white-feather tutu. She wound her long hair into a bun. After slipping her feet into her pointe shoes, she laced the silk straps up her calves. Then she made her way, *en pointe*, to the ballet studio.

Madame was waiting, her silver hair in its tight knot. She was long and lean, and stood on her red pointe shoes so that she seemed as tall and straight as a tree. Her expression was stern. She said not a word as Duchess crossed the floor and took her position at the barre. Then music began to play, and Duchess followed Madame's instructions. "First position. *Plié. Elevé.* Second position. *Plié. Elevé.*" And so it went, on and on.

It was hard work, but Duchess was used to it. She'd practiced every day since learning to walk, missing classes only when she'd been sick with childhood

illnesses such as pixie pox and fairy fever. Ballet required total focus and utmost dedication. It suited Duchess perfectly.

After two hours of *grand jétes*, pirouettes, and arabesques, Madame clapped her hands and the music stopped. Duchess grabbed a towel and dabbed sweat off her neck and shoulders.

"I can tell you have somezing on your mind," Madame said as she tapped her long fingers on the barre. "I watched zee MirrorCast zis morning. Is zis what you want? To be zee Next Top Villain?"

"I don't want to be a villain," Duchess said. "But Mr. Badwolf won't let me transfer. I don't know why he wants me in that class."

"Perhaps he recognizes potential in you," Madame said.

"Potential?" Duchess dabbed her forehead. "To be…*evil*? But it's my destiny to be the star of my story, not the villain."

Madame raised her penciled eyebrows. "Each of us has a light side and a dark side, Ms. Swan. Zee

question is not if you can win. Zee question is, will you choose to lose? Will you choose *defeat*?"

Duchess did not like that word—*defeat*. "Of course I won't choose to lose," she said. "But it's more complicated than that." She sat on a bench and began to untie her shoes.

"You are a ballerina, Ms. Swan. Ballerinas are unique creatures. We can do whatever we set our minds to do." Madame opened the studio door and pointed down the hallway. "Listen to zee other dancers," she said with disdain. "Zey are clomping around as zey attempt to learn zee common village dances. Zey do not possess our gracefulness. Zey do not defy gravity as we do." She crossed the room and towered over Duchess. "Why do you make zat frowny face?"

"Because I want to be the best student and the best ballerina, but I don't want to be the best villain."

"Zer is a light side and a dark side to ballet, no?"

"What do you mean?"

Madame spread her arms wide. "Zee light side of ballet is zee glory to be onstage. To have zee envy

of zee audience. And to hear zeir hands clapping in appreciation. *Oui?*"

"Yes," Duchess said, remembering the thrill of the rising curtain, the warmth of the spotlight, the thunder of applause. A shiver ran up her spine, then back down. How she loved those moments. Faces up-turned, eyes wide, watching her with envy.

Duchess removed her shoes and rested her tired feet on the floor. Madame pointed at Duchess's left foot, where a new blister had formed on the baby toe. "Zee dark side of ballet is zee physical pain. Zee countless hours of practice. Zee solitude."

Duchess nodded. While the village children played hide-and-seek, she'd spent many a day alone in the studio. And many a night bandaging her feet and soaking her aching muscles in salt baths. But nothing, not the pain or the solitude, could dis-courage her from perfecting her art.

"If you look deep inside, Ms. Swan, you will find zee determination you need to face zis challenge. A ballerina always meets her challenges."

Noise outside the windows drew their attention. Some students were walking past the studio, on their way to the Village of Book End. Lizzie, Madeline Hatter, and Kitty Cheshire, fellow Wonderlandians, were laughing and chatting, probably on their way to the Mad Hatter's Haberdashery & Tea Shoppe.

Then came a lone figure. It was Raven Queen. She was walking and reading a book at the same time. Her black hair sparkled in the sunlight. Duchess stepped close to the window. Raven didn't notice that she was being watched. She giggled as she read, then turned the page. She didn't look one bit worried about the General Villainy thronework. Why should she? She'd chosen to turn away from her responsibilities.

Madame's voice filled the studio. "When a ballerina no longer wants to dance the leading role, then another ballerina must step forward and take her place."

Duchess swallowed hard. "Take her place?"

"Are you going to turn your back on the leading role, Ms. Swan?"

Swan

Secrets

During a dinner of swamp greens and curly fries, Duchess felt as if the walls of the school were pressing in. She wanted to get away and think. So much had happened that day. Everyone was talking about the General Villainy thronework. Blondie Lockes had even painted a banner that read:

WHO WILL BE THE NEXT TOP VILLAIN?

She'd hung it from the Castleteria rafters.

Blondie interrupted Duchess's meal by trying to

interview her. "What mean and rotten thing are you going to do?" she asked, pushing her MirrorPad in front of Duchess's face. "And be sure to speak loud enough so everyone can hear you."

"It's not mean and rotten. It's rotten and nasty," Duchess corrected. "And even if I had a plan, why would I tell you?" She turned her back to the MirrorPad.

Blondie darted in front of her. "Are you saying you *don't* have a plan?"

"No, I'm not saying that." She tried to speak calmly so Blondie wouldn't suspect the truth.

Blondie spoke into her MirrorPad. "Well, people, you heard it here first. Duchess Swan says she's not saying she doesn't have a plan." Then Blondie hurried through the hall, trying to find another General Villainy student to interview.

Duchess quickly ate her meal. Then, with graceful steps, she slipped between onlookers and made her way outside. She could go to the ballet studio and

find solitude for her thoughts. But there was one other place where she could be alone.

After crawling into some shrubbery, Duchess closed her eyes and willed the transformation. Fortunately, the turning of arms into wings and mouth into beak was a painless process. Even the elongation of her neck didn't hurt. Another fortunate fact was that she didn't need to worry about her clothes. They magically disappeared, and reappeared on her body when she turned herself back into a human.

Transformation complete, she waddled out of the shrubs and jumped into her favorite Ever After High pond. Pirouette greeted her with a friendly nod, then went back to eating water bugs. The other swans were used to Duchess's intrusion. They didn't hiss at her or chase her away, as they did with other birds. Even though she was different from them, they allowed her to swim freely.

A unicorn statue stood in the center, spouting water from its horn. Water lilies covered the pond's surface. Duchess slowly paddled her webbed feet. The waxy, round leaves parted as she glided through.

This was a lovely way to spend the evening. But as much as she enjoyed these moments with Pirouette at her side, with the water below and the starlit sky above, she was completely aware that she did not want to be in this form forever after.

Stop thinking such things, she told herself. *You are not a Rebel like Raven.*

Students walked past, some holding hands, some in groups. They paid no attention to Duchess. To their eyes, she looked exactly like the other swans. And she paid no attention to her fellow students, until the scent of deliciousness tickled her beak.

Ginger sat on a bench at the side of the pond. She opened a box of pastries and tossed some crumbs into the water. Pirouette and the others rushed over and began to peck at the crumbs. Duchess wasn't hungry, and she was about to turn away when Ginger's MirrorPhone rang. Duchess wouldn't have eavesdropped, except she heard the word *thronework*.

She swam over, pretending to be interested in the soggy offerings.

"Yes, Mother, it's true, I'm supposed to do something rotten and nasty by the end of school on Friday." Ginger fidgeted on the bench. "I know, Mother. I don't want to disappoint you, but—" She sighed. "But—"

Ginger's mom kept interrupting. Duchess couldn't hear what she was saying, because her voice was muffled.

With the phone held to her ear, Ginger reached into the box and pulled out a moon pie. As she took a big bite, moonbeams shot out from between the layers of cake. "Yes, Mother, but—" Ginger chewed and nodded, listening to some sort of lecture. Duchess could only imagine: *Do what you're supposed to do. Uphold the family reputation. Do your duty.* Blah, blah, blah.

Two swans pushed against Duchess as they stretched their necks for more crumbs.

"Of course I have a plan, Mother." Ginger set the

moon pie back in the box. "I thought of it all by myself. On Wednesday morning, I'm going to sprinkle sandman powder onto my popular cinnamon trolls and serve them for breakfast. Then everyone will fall asleep and miss their first classes of the day." She smiled proudly, her teeth all chocolaty. "Then I'll wake everyone up with super-strong hocus lattes."

A shrieking sound burst out of the MirrorPhone's speaker.

"No, Mother, I don't need one of your recipes. I'm not going to poison anyone." Ginger waved at Ashlynn Ella, who was walking past. "Okay, gotta go, Mother. Bye!" Ginger tossed the rest of the crumbs into the pond, then hurried off to join her friends.

Sandman powder doesn't sound very evil, Duchess thought. And many students might be happy to miss their first class. With that sort of plan, Ginger surely wouldn't become the Next Top Villain. Duchess made a mental note to avoid the cinnamon trolls on Wednesday morning.

The problem remained—even though Ginger's

plan didn't sound terribly rotten and nasty, Duchess still needed a plan of her own.

It was getting late. More stars appeared in the sky. A group of cleaning fairies flew back toward the forest, leaving trails of blue and green glitter in their wake. Most of the students had headed indoors because it was time to get to bed. A good night's sleep was important for a ballerina, so Duchess swam to the edge of the pond and was about to step onto the damp grass when she heard familiar voices. Mr. Badwolf and Headmaster Grimm had stopped for a hushed conversation. Duchess floated into the tall reeds, then cocked her head, listening.

"I'm getting mirror calls from parents day and night," the headmaster said. "This Rebels nonsense has caused quite a stir. We're supposed to be teaching traditions here, not rebellion."

"We do our best," Mr. Badwolf said with a cough.

Duchess swam a bit closer. Then she straightened her neck so she could see over the tops of the reeds. As usual, Headmaster Grimm was dressed in a long

tailored wool jacket. A pocket watch hung from his waistcoat. He wrung his hands in a worried way. "The Charmings are threatening to send their children elsewhere if we don't get this situation under control. So is the Ella family. If we lose important royal families and their funding, we might have to close the school." His baritone voice was tight and higher than normal. "Educating the next Evil Queen is one of our most important duties."

"I'm afraid Raven Queen shows little interest," Mr. Badwolf said.

"Then we must begin to train someone to replace her, just in case. We need to be prepared." Headmaster Grimm stroked his gray mustache. "Do any of the students in your General Villainy class show promise?"

Mr. Badwolf growled. "Unfortunately, they are the most pathetic group I've ever taught. There's evil in their blood—no doubt about that—but they've diluted it with good intentions and...*generosity*." He coughed, as if the word had choked him. "Ginger

brought home-baked goodies to share." He growled again. "Ms. Swan kept asking to be transferred. Why did you insist that she take the class?"

Duchess nearly honked, she was so hexcited by this question. Would she finally get an answer? As she held perfectly still, Headmaster Grimm looked around. Then he cleared his throat and said, "This is highly classified information, Mr. Badwolf. But I believe, as do others, that Duchess Swan has a black swan side that might make her the perfect candidate for Evil Queen status."

"Black swan side?" Mr. Badwolf asked.

"Yes." Headmaster Grimm turned toward the pond and pointed to the swans that were swimming near the fountain. "The trumpeter is beautiful to behold, graceful and elegant, just like our Ms. Swan. But if you disturb a trumpeter, trespass through its territory, or threaten its nest, it will hiss like a cobra and attack with the viciousness of a wolf. That is the black swan side."

"And Duchess?"

"She has the instinct within her to do whatever it takes to protect her territory, and, in this case, her territory is her perfect grades. She will not allow herself to fail your challenge, Mr. Badwolf. She will do whatever it takes to succeed. Even if that means becoming a villain."

"Ah, I see," Mr. Badwolf said. "But what about her destiny? The swan princess is not a villain. By putting her in my class, are you not going against tradition? Are you not, in a small way, doing exactly what you don't want the students to do—choosing a new destiny?"

Headmaster Grimm snorted. "We are not Rebels, if that's what you're getting at, Mr. Badwolf. We are the upholders of tradition! Our stories depend upon an Evil Queen. And if Raven will not step into her mother's shoes, then someone else must. We cannot let those shoes go empty."

"Interesting."

"Have you noticed how Ms. Swan looks at the other students who have Happily Ever Afters? She

wants one desperately. If she passes General Villainy, then she'll move on to Advanced Villainy and begin to learn the dark spells. It wouldn't take her long to realize that by controlling dark magic, she could change the curse that awaits her."

Duchess's wings went limp with shock.

"If she changed the curse, then she wouldn't have to live her life as a bird." Mr. Badwolf nodded. "Now I understand. With that kind of motivation, how could she not want to become the Next Top Villain?"

"And once she has mastered dark magic, she may show the potential to be the next Evil Queen, saving all of us from the end of Ever After as we know it." The headmaster's voice faded as he and Mr. Badwolf walked away.

As the pond water lapped at her belly, Duchess floated, trying to understand what she'd just overheard. She could change her fate and Headmaster Grimm would approve?

But that would make her a . . . *Rebel*!

Duchess's

Decision

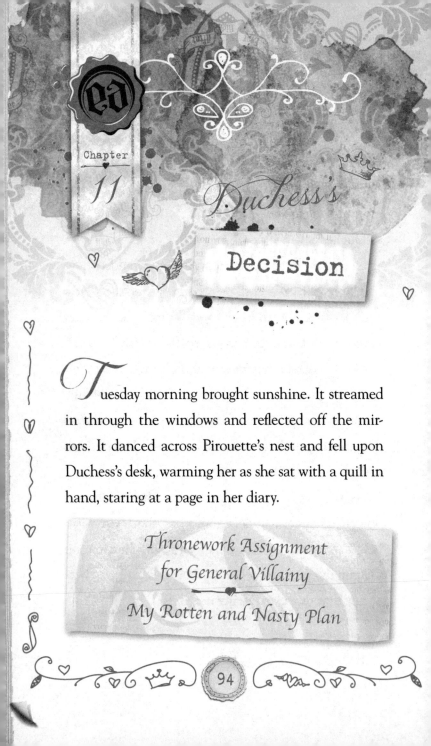

uesday morning brought sunshine. It streamed in through the windows and reflected off the mirrors. It danced across Pirouette's nest and fell upon Duchess's desk, warming her as she sat with a quill in hand, staring at a page in her diary.

*Thronework Assignment
for General Villainy*

My Rotten and Nasty Plan

The rest of the page was blank.

She dipped her quill into the ink. Even though she'd been sitting at that desk since dawn, no wicked plan had emerged. What could she do? The only magic she possessed was to turn herself into a swan. But hissing at people didn't seem very evil. And she didn't want to give the other swans a bad reputation and risk having them evicted from school property.

She scratched her head. A little white feather fell from her hair and onto the desk. It was a leftover from last night's transformation. Then she yawned. It had been a long, sleepless night. She'd stared, wide-eyed, at the wall, Headmaster Grimm's voice repeating in her mind.

She will do whatever it takes to succeed. Even if that means becoming a villain.

Duchess Swan had never been faced with such a dilemma. Her good grades had never been based on doing anything that resembled rebellion, or anything that went against her family's legacy. But now, if she

got the best grade in General Villainy, she'd be sent to Advanced Villainy and she'd work her way up the ladder of evil.

What would happen if she decided to quit? What if she flunked this class? Her evil career would be over. Headmaster Grimm would remove her from the list of potential candidates to take Raven's place. She'd never have to worry about villainy again. One fairy-fail grade on her transcript was not the end of the world, right?

But, by failing General Villainy, she would give up her opportunity to learn magic and change her fate. And she'd never get her Happily Ever After.

Oh feather duster! Talk about a lot to deal with. No wonder she was exhausted.

She turned back to the page in her diary, the one where she'd written...

I wish I had a Happily Ever After like Ashlynn's and Apple's.

"Lizzie?" she called.

Lizzie was still curled up in bed. "Hmmm?"

"Would you do *anything* for a Happily Ever After?" Duchess asked.

"Doing anything is much the same as doing everything or doing nothing, because they are all things." She was clearly still half asleep, her thoughts thick with Riddlish.

"Lizzie, I'm serious." Duchess turned and faced her roommate's bed. "If someone gave you the chance to be the kind of queen you wanted to be, and to live in Wonderland again, but in order to get those things you had to risk your reputation and your family's honor, would you take that chance?"

"Live in Wonderland again?" Lizzie bolted upright. Her hedgehog squeaked. "I would take that chance and every chance if it meant I could live happily in Wonderland."

Duchess nodded, then turned back to her desk. She and Lizzie wanted the same thing—a chance at happiness. And Headmaster Grimm was handing

Duchess her opportunity. All she had to do was take it. She squeezed the quill as she worked it out in her mind. Yes, this was what she'd prepared for. All those years of dedication and practice. She could do this. She would tell everyone that she was trying to keep her perfect grades. But secretly, she'd be on a new path, to a new destiny. She would never admit to anyone that she was being a Rebel.

The decision was made.

Plunk. An envelope landed on her desk. The fairy-godmother-in-training squeaked at her, then flew over to Lizzie's bed and dropped an envelope on her head.

"It's a delivery." Duchess picked up her envelope. The initials *HG* had been pressed into the center of the wax seal. "It's from Headmaster Grimm."

"Is that the time?" Lizzie asked after reading the wall clock. "How dare it move so quickly! Can you read the letter out loud?" She scrambled out of bed and dove into her closet. Duchess unfolded the envelope and read.

Dear General Villainy students,

I am pleased to report that news of your thronework assignment has spread far and wide—thanks to Ms. Lockes's *Just Right* MirrorCast.

I have heard from most of your families, and they are as eager as I to see you succeed. I do not need to remind you that every fairytale story needs a villain, so it is of the utmost importance that Ever After High continues to train and graduate villains of the highest evil standards.

I expect that you, the selected few, will become those future villains.

So on behalf of the entire Ever After High community and all the fairytale kingdoms, I wish you success in your thronework assignment. We are all looking forward to seeing who will be the Next Top Villain.

Sincerely,

Headmaster Grimm

"Talk about putting on the pressure," Duchess said. Then, so Lizzie wouldn't suspect her plan to win, she added, "This is the worst thronework ever."

"I've been wondering what to do," Lizzie said as she tossed pairs of socks over her head. "But doing and wondering are totally different things, and I'm not getting anywhere."

"Me neither," Duchess admitted as she closed her diary. Having no plan was worrisome, especially since it was Tuesday, and they had only until the end of the day Friday. No way was that enough time.

The dorm room door flew open, and Blondie Lockes stepped inside. "How is everyone feeling this morning?" she asked in her snoopy voice. Of course she was holding her MirrorPad, and the red recording light was on.

"Does no one in this dorm know how to knock?" Duchess asked. "Seriously. This school should offer a class."

"If I knocked, I would never get in anywhere," Blondie said.

She was right. Blondie's thirst for breaking news would stop Duchess from inviting her in. The girl would inevitably find a scoop, whether it was the mess flying out of Lizzie's closet or the feathers in Duchess's bed.

But even a locked door wouldn't keep Blondie out, because she possessed the magical ability to unlock doors with a simple touch of her hand.

"What do you want?" Duchess asked. She tucked Headmaster Grimm's letter into her desk drawer.

Blondie stepped over a pile of Lizzie's scepters, then plopped onto a heart-shaped beanbag chair. "Do you know how many hits I got on my Mirror-Cast yesterday?"

Duchess scowled at her. "Oh, how rude of me," she said sarcastically. "Do make yourself at home."

"Thanks," Blondie said. She wiggled her rump until the beanbag chair fit just right. "Anyhoo, the Next Top Villain episode was the most-watched since I uncovered the alarming fact that the Castleteria's peas porridge is nine days old. You guys are famous!"

A belt whizzed past Blondie's head. "In Wonderland, a princess *never* has to find her own clothes!" Lizzie cried from the closet.

Blondie tousled her locks, then smiled at Duchess. "So? Have you made your rotten and nasty plan? What is it? I must know."

Duchess dumped kibble into Pirouette's bowl. "In case you haven't noticed, Blondie, I get the best grades in school, which means I'm pretty smart. So why would I tell you anything?"

Blondie sighed. "You can't blame me for trying." She pointed her MirrorPad at the closet. "What about you, Lizzie? What are you going to do for your Villainy thronework?"

Lizzie emerged, fully dressed, except that she'd put her hedgehog on her head instead of a hat. "I don't know what I'm going to do," she said. Then she looked around. "Where's Shuffle?"

"Well, looks like there's nothing here for me to report. And I've got an episode to air." Blondie hurried from the room, MirrorPad in hand. "See ya."

For a brief moment, Duchess felt relieved that she wasn't the only one who didn't have a rotten and nasty plan. But that didn't solve anything.

It took a few more minutes for Lizzie to get herself put together. Then she and Duchess headed out to grab a quick breakfast before the first class of the day. As they walked through the Common Room, a morning special edition of *Just Right* was already under way. Blondie's face filled all the mirrors. "When asked about the General Villainy thronework, Lizzie Hearts said this."

The report cut to footage of Lizzie standing with her hedgehog on her head, saying, "I don't know what I'm going to do."

Then the report cut back to Blondie. "Well, you heard it here first, people. Lizzie Hearts doesn't know what she's going to do. Could Lizzie be out before she's even begun? Could this be the end for her? Stay tuned for more details as they emerge."

"Oh, what a mean thing to say. I'd like to turn her into a croquet ball!" Lizzie said with a stomp of

her foot. "How can I be out before I've even begun? That's total nonsense. I've begun at the beginning, and everyone knows that the beginning is where you begin and not where you end." She swung her book bag over her shoulder. Then she plucked Shuffle from her head. "That Blondie should be in General Villainy class."

Duchess wondered if she should take a clue from Blondie. Gossip could be hurtful and do more harm than good. Sometimes it was downright evil. Maybe that could be her thronework—to create a rumor. It was worth thinking about.

Blondie's MirrorCast wasn't over. "In other news, Daring Charming is looking for a personal shopper. If you'd like to apply for the job—"

Shrieks and squeals filled the air as half the female population ran from the building in search of Daring.

As Apple White and Ashlynn Ella walked past, Apple said, "When Daring and I have our Happily

Ever After, we are obviously going to need an entire castle just for closet space." They both giggled.

For once, Duchess did not feel envious of Apple. Apple was imagining her carefree life with her future Prince Charming. Her Happily Ever After.

Because Duchess was imagining her own.

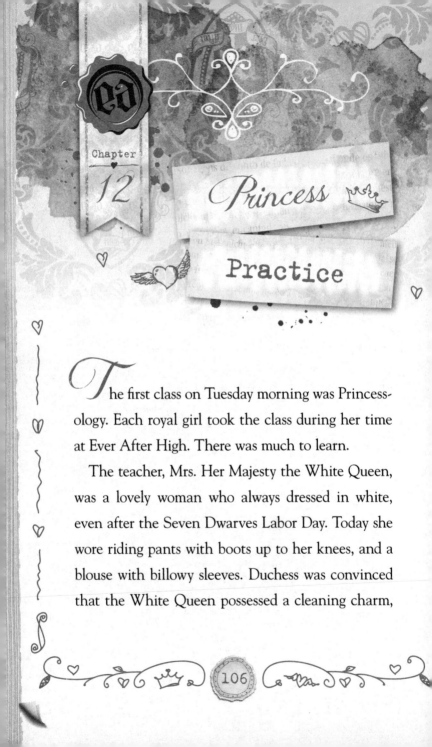

Princess

Practice

The first class on Tuesday morning was Princessology. Each royal girl took the class during her time at Ever After High. There was much to learn.

The teacher, Mrs. Her Majesty the White Queen, was a lovely woman who always dressed in white, even after the Seven Dwarves Labor Day. Today she wore riding pants with boots up to her knees, and a blouse with billowy sleeves. Duchess was convinced that the White Queen possessed a cleaning charm, for never did a single speck of dirt or an oily splotch mar the pure whiteness of her attire.

"Good morning, princesses," she said. Then she pressed a finger to her pointed chin. "Though I wonder, is it necessary to call a morning *good*? Does it not go without saying that all mornings are good, for to be without a morning would be very bad indeed." She was from Wonderland, so like Lizzie, she often said way more words than were necessary.

"Good morning," the princesses replied as they took their places in the grandstand at the edge of the athletic field. The field itself had been transformed. There were all sorts of strange objects and people standing in the middle of it. What was going on?

Duchess and Lizzie sat on a bench. Ashlynn Ella and Apple White sat on another. Other students included Briar Beauty, daughter of Sleeping Beauty; Darling Charming, sister to Daring; and Poppy and Holly O'Hair, daughters of Rapunzel. Blondie Lockes was there, too, even though she'd never proved her royal heritage. And, of course, last but not least, sitting solo, was Raven Queen.

"What in Ever After are we doing out here?" Briar asked as she pulled down her ever-present pair of crownglasses to shield her eyes.

"It's so very sunny," Apple chirped. She pulled out a bottle of sunscreen and began to apply it to her arms so thickly it looked like she was frosting a cake. "I'm called the Fairest One of All because I'm *literally* the fairest."

"Taking care of your skin is a very princess thing to do," Mrs. Her Majesty said approvingly. Then she clapped her hands. "Now, ladies, we are outside because our lesson cannot be taught in a classroom."

"I'm so glad we're outside today," Ashlynn Ella said. A pair of songbirds were weaving a braid in her hair. "Are we going to take a walk in the woods? A deer told me that a new family of raccoons has moved in. Shall we go and visit them?"

Mrs. Her Majesty made a *tsk-tsk* sound. "Ms. Ella, my dear, I appreciate your love of the woodland

creatures, but a princess should never socialize with rodents. Alice made this mistake when she befriended the March Hare and the Dormouse."

"Raccoons aren't rodents," Ashlynn said.

"But of course they are. How very silly of you not to know that." Mrs. Her Majesty gave Ashlynn a pitiful look. "A masked face does not hide the rodent nature that lies inside."

Duchess wondered if she might make raccoons part of her rotten and nasty plan.

Mrs. Her Majesty clapped her hands again. "Young ladies, the purpose of Princessology is to prepare you, the next generation of royal damsels, for your futures as queens. Therefore, we will be learning a variety of important skills. One of the most important is how to travel like a princess."

"Oooh, I love to travel. Where are we going?"

"My family has a private pumpkin."

"I took a mermaid cruise once. That was amazing!"

"Have you ever chartered a Pegasus? That is seriously awesome."

"Ladies, please do not interrupt. Interrupting is not becoming of a princess." Mrs. Her Majesty pursed her thin lips. "We teach traditional values here at Ever After High. And the most traditional way to travel is on horseback. A princess should therefore be a skilled equestrian."

Some of the princesses groaned, including Lizzie. "I don't want to ride a horse," she announced. "They never obey my orders. The last time I rode one, it kept stopping to eat my mother's roses."

"Riding on horseback offers its advantages, Ms. Hearts. It protects you from stepping in unpleasant things and thus keeps your dainty slippers clean and tidy."

Lizzie folded her arms. "My mother never steps in anything unpleasant. She orders her card soldiers to chop everything down and sweep a clear path wherever she goes. And that's what I'm going to do, too."

"That sounds like a hexcellent plan, Ms. Hearts, but in the meantime, as this is not Wonderland, and

you are not yet queen, you will attend to your duties here at Ever After High. And one of those duties is mastering your equestrian skills."

Lizzie grumbled to herself. Duchess wished that time would move faster. She was eager to end this class so she could begin to work on her Villainy plan.

Mrs. Her Majesty the White Queen pointed into the field. "Behind me is your obstacle course. Today we will practice riding through it. And on Friday you will be tested on your skills. This thronework assignment is very important in your paths to becoming perfect princesses." She smiled.

"Friday?" both Duchess and Lizzie blurted.

Blondie Lockes grabbed her MirrorPad, pressed the record button, and shot over to their bench. "News flash. Duchess, Lizzie, and Raven now face two major thronework assignments, both due this Friday. How does that make you feel? Are you feeling stressed?"

"The only thing making me stressed is you," Lizzie said, pushing the MirrorPad away from her face.

Duchess felt as if a thick, smothering blanket had just been flung over her. Two huge assignments both due by the week's end. She glanced at Raven, who sat with her feet on the bench, her arms wrapped around her legs. Raven looked back at Duchess, her jaw clenched. Was she also feeling the pressure?

It would be so easy for Raven to win Next Top Villain. She already possessed magic, though her spells often backfired. But if she put her mind to it, she could conjure storm clouds and flood the school, or summon a flock of ravens to poop on everyone's heads. She simply had to choose to not be a Rebel.

A Rebel, like Duchess.

Horse

Course

The horses were led from the stable and out to the grandstand. Each wore a saddle that matched a princess's signature colors. Duchess's was white and black with lavender accents.

Duchess knew how to ride. Her balance was impeccable, and she thought of the relationship between the rider and the horse as a sort of *pas de deux*. That was, until she discovered how easily horses startle. At age nine, she'd been out for a ride and a pair of trumpeters had flown overhead, approaching the pond for a landing. Her horse had reared, and she'd been thrown. Luckily no bones were broken and she'd been able to dance the next day. But Duchess never forgot the horse's kicking back legs and its fearful whinny. Though she mastered her equestrian skills, she never fully trusted the creatures again.

The princesses were introduced to their horses. Raven's was jet-black and larger than the others. Its eyes were as red as burning embers. "Uh, my horse looks kinda evil," Raven said nervously. It stomped its front hoof as if agreeing.

Ashlynn started making snorting sounds as she talked to her horse. Then, both she and the horse started laughing.

Apple fed her horse a red apple, which she just happened to have in her book bag. And everyone else patted her horse's head and said hello.

Duchess ran a hand over her horse's silky mane. "As long as you don't toss me off your back, we'll get along just fine," she told it.

"Ladies," Mrs. Her Majesty called. She was already

seated on a beautiful white horse. She held a riding crop in one hand and a megaphone in the other. "Mount your horses, and I shall lead you through the obstacle course. And remember, a princess always rides sidesaddle."

It took Lizzie five tries before she could sit on the saddle and not fall off. "Why can't we play croquet?" she asked, wobbling. "Somebody make this horse stand still!"

Although Duchess had no trouble getting on the horse, she was having a difficult time paying attention. *I need a rotten and nasty plan.*

Mrs. Her Majesty led the princesses toward the field. She spoke into her megaphone. "This is the starting point." A sign read: START HERE. "You will then follow the golden path." She pointed to the ground where a path had been created out of gold-colored sawdust. "Stay to this path until you reach the end, and you will succeed. Veer off the path, and you will fairy-fail." With a flick of her riding crop, she moved up the path until she reached some people. "Your first obstacle will be an adoring crowd." A group of villagers stood in a clump. They weren't actual villagers. Duchess recognized a few of them from the Castleteria kitchen. But they were dressed in costumes and held bouquets of flowers and autograph books. They cheered as the princesses neared. "Always wave and smile." Mrs. Her Majesty demonstrated.

"This is easy," Holly O'Hair said. "I'm used to being up high and waving at people."

Duchess also thought it was easy, but Lizzie was wobbling in the saddle and holding on to the reins for dear life.

Mrs. Her Majesty led them to another group of people. "Next, you will be greeted by an angry crowd." The costumed "villagers" were now holding rakes and baskets of rotten fruit, which they proceeded to toss.

"Hey!" Lizzie said. "Stop that! I order you to stop that!"

"Why are they throwing things?" Apple said as a

mold-covered strawberry whizzed past her head. "My subjects would never be angry with me. I love each and every one of them." It was well known that the people in Apple White's kingdom wore I ♥ APPLE shirts.

"A princess must always be prepared," Mrs. Her Majesty said as she kicked her horse into a canter. "One never knows which way the wind may blow. One day you're beloved, the next day you're despised."

One day you're a Royal, the next day you're a Rebel, Duchess thought as she wiped a piece of pear from her face.

And so it went. The princesses followed Mrs. Her Majesty the White Queen as she led them around the obstacle course, instructing them on the proper procedure. There were heaps of dragon dung to avoid. There was a moat to cross and an old crone to ignore.

They came to a bridge that was guarded by a cranky troll. Tiny, a giant, had dug a deep ravine beneath the bridge, and the troll threatened to push anyone who tried to cross. When he blocked Lizzie's path, she bonked him on the head with her scepter.

"Dear, oh dear, Ms. Hearts. That is not the correct way to deal with a troll bridge," Mrs. Her Majesty said. "A princess never defends herself. You must always call for a prince to rescue you."

"I was going to jump the ravine, but okay," Briar said. She stopped her horse in front of a tree, upon which hung a red phone. EMERGENCY PRINCE PATROL. Briar picked up the receiver. "Yes, hello, there's this troll guy here and he's guarding this bridge, and I need to get across it." She listened, then put down the receiver. "Um, the prince on duty says he's in the middle of downloading the latest version of *Dragon Conquest Sixteen*, and he can't leave or he'll have to start all over again."

Mrs. Her Majesty scowled. "That is unacceptable. Give me that phone!" She yanked it from Briar's hand and began to give the unfortunate prince a very stern lecture about his duties.

The princesses took this opportunity to dismount and stretch their legs. With her horse in tow, Blondie slid right up next to Duchess. "So, Duchess, are you worried about having two major assignments due on Friday? Will you be able to keep up your perfect grades? Is there anything you'd like to say to the *Just Right* audience?"

"I'm not worried," Duchess lied. "I know how to ride a horse."

"Yes, but do you know how to be evil?" Blondie's golden horse matched her golden hair. It turned its head and sniffed Duchess's face in a real snoopy way. "Are you thinking of dropping out of the Next Top Villain competition?" Blondie held up her MirrorPad, waiting for the answer. The horse raised its eyebrows, as if also waiting.

"I don't drop out of things," Duchess said calmly. "So there's no scoop here, Blondie."

"Why are you in General Villainy class, anyway?" Blondie asked. "Everyone knows you don't have evil in your bloodline. Is there some sort of secret that you're hiding from the rest of us?" She put her face close to Duchess's. "If you ask me, I think you've got some royally serious competition. I mean, you're going up against Raven. If she donated blood, the packet would be labeled *Type Evil.*"

Duchess was about to tell Blondie that no one had asked her opinion, but a loud screeching sound arose from the forest, as if a giant were scratching his nails on a humongous chalkboard. Which was possible.

The horses went berserk, neighing and kicking their back legs. Only Mrs. Her Majesty the White Queen was still mounted, and she expertly slid off the saddle, the Prince Patrol phone left dangling from the tree. The horses galloped back toward the stable. "What-ever-after is that wretched noise?" she asked.

"It's Sparrow Hood," Raven said. "He's playing his guitar." The screeching continued.

"That is *not* muse-ic to my ears," Mrs. Her Majesty said. "The horses are stampeding! Someone must tell him to stop."

"I'll do it," Duchess volunteered. It occurred to her that Blondie was right. If Raven set her mind to it, she'd win Next Top Villain in a heartbeat. Duchess needed help. "I'll go tell Sparrow to stop playing."

She didn't care whether or not Sparrow played his muse-ic. But he had made her an offer. And since she'd come up with nothing better, perhaps it was time to discuss a partnership. Duchess raced toward the forest.

"Tell young Mr. Hood that I intend to file a complaint!" Mrs. Her Majesty hollered through the megaphone. "Princesses have extremely delicate eardrums."

As soon as Duchess had entered the forest and was out of view, she closed her eyes and took to the sky.

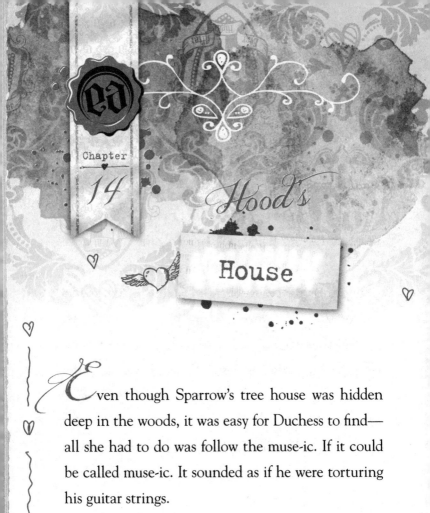

Even though Sparrow's tree house was hidden deep in the woods, it was easy for Duchess to find—all she had to do was follow the muse-ic. If it could be called muse-ic. It sounded as if he were torturing his guitar strings.

She dove between branches, landing in a clearing. Because the trees grew so thick in this part of the forest, she'd have to walk on foot the rest of the way.

The screeching grew louder and louder. A pair of

deer raced past, trying to outrun the noise. Flocks
of birds shot out of the treetops, desperately making
their escape.

And there it was, a tree house like no other she'd
seen, perched at the tops of two massive fir trees. It
had been built from a hodgepodge of materials—
old doors and window frames, leftover siding from
barns and cabins. There was even a hull from an old
boat. Duchess began to climb the wooden staircase
that wound around and around one of the trunks.
Sparrow didn't live in the dormitory with the other
boy students. He'd claimed this space as his own. He
was an outsider who didn't seem to care about fitting
in. He didn't care about grades or hexpectations or
any of the stuff that ruled her days. Sparrow Hood
cared about his muse-ic. And *himself*. Which was
why she would need to proceed carefully.

A bow and a quiver of arrows hung from a hook
at the entry. An envelope with a wax seal sat on the
faded welcome mat. Sparrow had gotten the same
letter from Headmaster Grimm, but he hadn't read

it yet. She picked it up. "Hello?" she called. Guitar sounds blasted from the open doorway. He'd never hear her above the racket, so she stepped inside. The floorboards vibrated.

Sparrow was standing on a small stage, a microphone perched on a stand. His guitar was plugged into an amp. He strummed furiously, and Duchess thought her eardrums might start bleeding.

"Hello?" She picked up a pillow and threw it at him.

The pillow bounced off his guitar, and he stopped playing. "Hey," he said, pulling earphones off his head and tossing them aside. "What's up? Did you come here to buy my demo?"

She stepped across the faded rug. The decor was what some might call rocker. She would never want to live in such a mess. The beanbag chairs were patched and faded, and the old couch leaked stuffing. Soda cans and latte cups lay everywhere, as did a thick coat of dust. Sparrow desperately needed an army of cleaning fairies.

"Mrs. Her Majesty the White Queen sent me to

tell you to stop playing," Duchess told him. "You're disturbing the horses."

"Horses?" He frowned. "Since when do I care about horses? I'm practicing my art."

"I know, but not everyone appreciates your...*art*," Duchess said. She handed him the envelope. "It's from Headmaster Grimm."

"So?" He slumped onto the couch and stretched out his legs, resting his bare feet on a wooden crate that served as a table.

"You should read it," she said. "It's important."

He groaned, then broke the seal and read the letter from the headmaster. "Blah, blah, blah," he said. "He wants us to become villains because our fairytale lives need villains. Yadda, yadda, yadda." He crumpled the parchment and tossed it over his shoulder. "Why'd you come here? Anyone could have told me that my muse-ic is too loud."

She pushed aside some empty chip bags and sat on the edge of the couch. "I came here to talk to you," she told him.

125

"About?" He smiled wickedly.

She frowned. "About our thronework assignment. About winning this Next Top Villain thing. About us working together—*maybe* working together. I still need to think about it."

He folded his arms behind his head. "What's to think about? You want the grade and the title. I just want a piece of treasure from Mr. Badwolf's vault. If I knew how to unravel security passwords, I'd break in and steal a couple of those golden arrows myself."

Duchess glanced around the tree house, to make sure none of Sparrow's Merry Men band members was hanging out. She and Sparrow appeared to be alone. "I heard the headmaster talking to Mr. Badwolf. He put me in the class because he thinks I have a black swan side to me."

"That surprised you?"

"Don't you get it? He thinks I have potential to *take Raven's place*." Her mouth suddenly felt dry. Sharing her feelings with Sparrow was risky, but

she needed someone to talk to. He wasn't a Royal, so he wouldn't judge her the way the other Royals might, including Lizzie. "He said that if I got an A in General Villainy, and then moved on to Advanced Villainy, I'd have a chance to learn magic."

"And with magic, you could change your cruddy destiny."

Her eyes welled with tears. Hearing someone else say it made it feel even more real.

"Well, if I were you and I had to choose between being a duck for the rest of my life or being a human, I'd choose human, obviously. Because a duck cannot play the guitar."

"Swan," she corrected as she wiped a stray tear.

"Seems to me we need to win this thing so you can always be a girl and I can get my treasure." Sparrow walked into the kitchen and grabbed a couple of fairycherry sodas from the fridge. He handed her one, then plopped down next to her on the couch. After a long sip, he wiped his mouth with his hand and said, "What's our plan?"

The fairycherry soda was refreshing, and it helped calm her nerves. She'd never felt this anxious, not even before stepping onstage to do a solo performance. This was a big decision. This would change her life. It would change the way people looked at her. It would change her place in the universe.

"Raven is our competition because she has evil in her blood. The only thing I do well is ballet and turning myself into a swan." She took another drink. "Oh, and I know that Ginger is going to put sandman powder into the cinnamon trolls tomorrow morning."

"How do you know this?"

"I heard her talking."

"Did she see you?"

"No, I was swimming with the other swans."

He smiled. "So that's your advantage. You can turn into a swan and eavesdrop because no one knows it's you. Then you can find out what everyone is planning and sabotage it."

"And what's your advantage?" she asked.

"My laziness. I'm going to help you by not doing anything." He moved to a beanbag chair and stretched across it. "I don't care if I fairy-fail, and sabotage sounds like way too much work."

"But..." She set her soda on the crate. "I don't understand. I thought you wanted to work together on this."

"Relax. We will be working together. I won't do the thronework. That way, you only have four other students to compete with. I'm increasing your chance of success by... by..." He scratched his head.

"One-fifth."

"Right. And then, when you win, my little reward will be the treasure vault."

She held up a hand. "Hold on a minute. This isn't really a partnership. You weren't going to do the thronework anyway."

"It's a partnership because you didn't have a plan, and now you do, thanks to *moi*." He beat his hands on the beanbag chair as if it were a drum.

She narrowed her eyes. "So let me get this straight.

My rotten and nasty plan is to ruin everyone else's rotten and nasty plans."

"Exactamundo. You're as sharp as an arrow."

"But do you think ruining other plans is enough?"

"Eavesdropping and sabotage are totally evil," he said with a smirk. "And don't forget, you'll have to double-cross a friend."

"A friend?" She inhaled sharply. In addition to Raven's, Ginger's, and Faybelle's plans, Duchess would have to sabotage Lizzie's as well. She clenched her jaw. Lizzie would never forgive her. And then Duchess would probably lose the only friend she had at Ever After High. "I don't know if I can do that."

He took another sip. "Hey, you know my dad's motto, 'Rob from the rich and give to the poor'? Well, in your case, it would be 'Rob from the other students and give to yourself.'" He snorted. "Oh, awesome. Did you see that? Soda just came out of my nose."

But Duchess wasn't looking at Sparrow's nose. She was looking at her future—one with two human legs.

Sweet

Sabotage

t was early Wednesday morning when Duchess slipped out of bed. Without lighting a candle or a lamp, she dressed quickly, choosing a pair of ballet slippers so there'd be no loud footsteps. Her legs felt wobbly, but whether it was due to nervousness or hexcitement, she wasn't sure. Lizzie and her hedgehog were still snoring as Duchess tied a cape around her neck. She pulled the hood over her head, then tucked a stray lavender lock inside. After silently opening the window for Pirouette, she

sneaked out of the room and down the hall. The girls' dormitory was silent. Even the trees seemed asleep. At some point the night before, Blondie had strung another banner from wall to wall.

WHO WILL WIN THE NEXT TOP VILLAIN? WATCH **JUST RIGHT** FOR THE LATEST SCOOP.

Duchess rolled her eyes. Who would have thought a thronework assignment would get so much attention?

Quietly, she opened the dormitory's front door and slipped outside. A few lingering stars twinkled, waiting for dawn to erase them from the cloudless sky. As she hurried toward one of the classroom buildings, the dewy ground soaked into her shoes, and a morning chill cut through her cape. She shivered, pulling it tighter. No one was out and about. The groundskeepers hadn't yet arrived, nor had any of the delivery vans. Students weren't supposed to leave the dorm from midnight to 6:00 AM.

Maybe Mr. Badwolf would give her hextra credit for breaking a rule.

She shivered again. *You can do this*, she told herself. *Don't be scared.*

When she reached the building's entrance, she glanced around to make sure she'd gone unnoticed. A cat watched from an upstairs window, its eyes half closed in a lazy way. But the other windows were dark and empty. The coast appeared clear, so, with a gentle push, Duchess opened the door and entered the building. She crept down the hall until she reached the classroom she'd been seeking. The sign read: COOKING CLASS-IC.

Thanks to her *Spells Kitchen* show, everyone at Ever After High knew that Ginger Breadhouse liked to cook. At first, many felt suspicious of her. After all, her mother was the Candy Witch, who used her sweets for wicked purposes. But it hadn't taken long for Ginger to make her mark as an extraordinary baker and candy-maker. Ginger's magic touch was the ability to turn anything into something delicious.

Duchess knew that if Ginger was creating goodies for her General Villainy thronework assignment, this classroom was where she'd make them.

Once inside, Duchess took a long, deep breath, filling her nostrils with the heavenly aroma. The shelves were lined with clear glass jars, each one filled with yummy things such as gumdrops, peppermint sticks, and candy buttons. The spice rack sat next to the sprinkle rack, which sat next to the frosting rack and the apron rack. Baking pots and pans hung from the ceiling, and cookie cutters were strewn everywhere. The scent of sweetness was so thick that Duchess imagined she could eat the air. Her stomach growled.

She walked to the center of the room, where a dozen rows of cinnamon trolls were lying on a long oak table. Ginger must have baked late into the night.

And there it was. A tiny bottle labeled: SANDMAN POWDER. The seal had not yet been broken. Duchess grabbed it, uncorked the lid, and shook the sand into a sink as quickly as she could, careful not to

inhale any of the grains or get them on her skin. She rinsed it all carefully down the drain. She had to hurry. Dawn was beginning to tickle the windows, and Ginger might arrive at any moment. What could she use to refill the bottle? Flour didn't seem right, and all the candy sprinkles were tinted. She found a canister of sugar. That should do it. Just as she finished refilling the bottle, a creak startled her. She whipped around.

Ginger was walking through the door. Duchess gasped, but it came out as a honk.

"Duchess, is that you?" Ginger stepped inside. "What a sweet surprise. What are you doing here?"

"Uh…" Duchess tucked her hand behind her back, the little bottle in her clutches.

Ginger smiled. Then she pushed her pink glasses up her nose. "I bet you came in because you smelled the cinnamon trolls."

She was so nice she didn't suspect a thing. *How can she be related to the Candy Witch?* Duchess wondered. *Maybe she was adopted.*

135

"Yep," Duchess said. "That's why I'm here. They smell great."

Ginger tied a pink polka-dot apron around her waist. "You want one? Help yourself. But just to warn you"—she grabbed a wooden spoon—"they don't have the cinnamon icing yet. I was going to make it this morning. When I'm finished, I'm going to take these to the Castleteria and hand them out. Can you help me?"

"I guess so." Duchess looked around. Where was that tiny cork for the bottle?

Ginger opened a tub of white frosting. "But after I ice them, don't eat any until we get to the Castleteria. I don't want you to fall asleep." She bit her lower lip. "Oops. I didn't mean that. Because why would someone fall asleep after eating one of my trolls? Unless they went into a sugar stupor." She giggled nervously.

Duchess pretended not to notice Ginger's discomfort. She spotted the cork sitting by the sink

and took a few steps backward, reaching carefully so Ginger wouldn't see.

When Ginger turned to grab a tin from the spice rack, Duchess quickly corked the bottle, now filled with sugar, and set it on the table.

"Here's the cinnamon," Ginger said, opening the tin. As she shook the spice into the frosting bowl, a cloud of cinnamon rose and drifted overhead. "And then I add my super-secret ingredient." She looked around. "There it is." While humming the sleepy lullaby "Rock-a-Bye Baby," she uncorked the tiny bottle and dumped it into the frosting. Then she stirred with the wooden spoon, a big smile on her face.

It was a little eerie.

After frosting each troll, Duchess and Ginger carried the trays from the classroom. Ginger stopped at the teachers' lounge and knocked on the door. "Is Mr. Badwolf here?" she asked when Professor Poppa Bear, the Beast Training and Care teacher, stuck out his head.

"Yum. Are those trolls for me?" He reached out a big, furry paw, but Ginger stepped away. "No, they're definitely not for the teachers. I need to talk to Mr. Badwolf." Duchess stood across the hall, watching.

"Hey, Badwolf! You got a visitor!"

"Hello, Ms. Breadhouse," Mr. Badwolf said. He moved his carved smoking pipe to the side of his mouth. "What do you want?"

"Could you come to the Castleteria?" she asked. "I'm going to do my thronework assignment for General Villainy, and I wanted you to see it."

He reached out to grab a troll, but she pulled away. "Oh no, Mr. Badwolf, don't eat one of those. I…" She glanced over her shoulder, then whispered, "I used a different recipe."

Mr. Badwolf smiled wickedly, showing off his razor-sharp canines. "It appears to me, Ms. Bread-house, that you are using your cooking skills in this assignment. How very promising. Yes, I shall accompany you in order to witness the results of your thronework." He tucked his pipe into his vest pocket, then closed the teachers' lounge door behind him. "Ms. Swan," he said as he looked across the hallway, "are you part of this evilness?"

"No," Duchess replied. "I'm just helping Ginger carry these trays."

He growled. "How very disappointing. Being helpful is not villainous."

That's what you think.

Students were streaming into the Castleteria. The morning Mirrornews was under way. "Good morning, Ever After High students. Today's weather forecast is sunny-ever-after, with a one hundred percent possibility of rainbows. The Castleteria breakfast special is a choice of porridge, gruel, or bran flakes."

Most of the students grumbled with disappointment. Porridge and gruel were the traditional way to begin the fairytale day, but the only student who seemed to like the stuff was Blondie Lockes.

"I brought cinnamon trolls!" Ginger announced.

Just like the swans in the pond who'd raced to eat

Ginger's crumbs, the students went berserk, pushing and shoving to get to the trays. It was a feeding frenzy! In the wink of an eye, the trays were emptied and everyone in the vicinity, except for Duchess, Ginger, and Mr. Badwolf, had sticky fingers. "Watch what happens," Ginger told Mr. Badwolf with a nudge. "It's going to get me an A for sure."

Pastries were consumed. Fingers were licked clean. Tea was poured, and the Castleteria was once again filled with conversation and activity.

Mr. Badwolf tapped his shoe, then checked his wristwatch. "Is something going to happen, Ms. Breadhouse?"

Ginger cupped her hands and hollered, "Doesn't anyone feel sleepy?"

"I always feel sleepy," Briar said as she walked past. "But that cinnamon troll gave me a sugar rush. I'm ready to party."

Mr. Badwolf's hair bristled. "Is this your idea of rotten and nasty?" he asked Ginger. "Giving everyone a *sugar rush*?"

"No," Ginger said frantically. "I put sandman powder in the icing. Everyone is supposed to fall asleep and miss class."

"*Supposed to* does not count," he said as he whipped out his clipboard. "You earn a fairy-fail, Ms. Breadhouse. I only hope my other students don't disappoint me as much as you have."

Faybelle swooped over, landing right next to Mr. Badwolf, her little silver wings flapping in double time thanks to her sugar rush. "I won't disappoint you," she said with a confident smile. "I've got my plan, and it'll be stupendously rotten. Give me an *R*. Give me an *O*. Give me a *T*. Give me another *T*. Give—"

"I look forward to it," Mr. Badwolf interrupted. Then he strode back to the teachers' lounge.

Duchess knew Ginger had worked hard, and she felt a little bad about the sabotage. But Ginger didn't seem too unhappy. She just shrugged and said, "Oh well. At least everyone likes my baking."

One down, Duchess thought as Ginger skipped

away. And it hadn't been too hard to accomplish. Hopefully, the others would be as easy.

Her stomach growled. Who knew that sneaking out before dawn and upsetting someone else's thronework would work up such an appetite? But as she grabbed a double helping of porridge, Blondie's face filled the mirrors.

"Hello, fellow fairytales. Don't rush off to class just yet, because I've got the latest scoop for you." The theme muse-ic for *Just Right* blasted from the speakers. Blondie demanded attention, and she always got it. "I know everyone is talking about the Next Top Villain. After all, I'm the one who came up with that catchy little title. And look, people, Sparrow Hood wrote a theme song."

Sparrow appeared on the mirror, and everyone stuck their fingers in their ears as his guitar blasted from the speakers. *"They're so evil,"* he sang. *"They're so awful. They're so rotten they're unlawful. Can't wait to see, who will be, Next Top Villain! The NEXT"*—scream—*"TOP"*—scream—*"VILLAIN!"*

The camera cut back to Blondie, who was holding a sheet of paper in her hand. "This just in: Two of the contestants have been eliminated."

Two? Duchess thought.

"Ginger's attempt to cast an evil spell on the students of Ever After High went horribly wrong this morning. Looks like Ginger's a big fairy-fail. And I've got the exclusive on Sparrow Hood. He told me that he's not going to bother with the thronework. So that's an automatic fairy-fail."

Six photos appeared on the screen, one of each General Villainy student. Ginger's face had a gold X over it. So did Sparrow's.

"That leaves four students still in the running. But three of them—Lizzie, Raven, and Duchess—have double thronework. Will one of them quit under the pressure? Will it be...Lizzie? Stay tuned.

And remember, if it's not too hot or too cold, it must be *Just Right*." Then the mirrors went dark.

Duchess dumped some fairyberries onto her porridge. Sparrow had kept his end of the agreement, and she was keeping hers. She smiled to herself as she ate. Success actually made the porridge taste better. Maybe this whole villain thing wouldn't be so difficult after all. Maybe this was the beginning of a new The End.

A sharp breeze blew through Duchess's hair as Faybelle flew past. The cheerhexer had a sneaky look on her face.

Duchess scrambled off the bench and followed. Two down, three more to go.

he Ever After High cheerhexing squad, composed mostly of fairies, had gathered near the croquet field, since the athletic field was still covered by the Princessology obstacle course. The cheerhexers wore matching Ever After High uniforms and carried pom-poms. As quickly as possible, Duchess ducked behind one of the equipment sheds and transformed. Then she flew over a fence and landed in the middle of the flamingo pen.

The flamingos belonged to Lizzie. As captain of

Ever After High's croquet team, Lizzie insisted on playing the Wonderland version of the game. This meant that ordinary wooden mallets were replaced by flamingos, and traditional croquet balls were replaced by rolled-up hedgehogs. No one got hurt in the process. The critters seemed to love the game as much as Lizzie.

Because it was naptime, each of the flamingos stood perched on one leg, beak tucked beneath wing. There was no way for Duchess to blend in. She was as white as snow, while the flamingos were as pink as cotton candy. Also, Duchess's swan legs weren't as long as the flamingos', but her ballet training helped her to hold *passé* as long as she needed. None of the cheerhexers noticed the out-of-place swan. But they probably wouldn't have noticed a dragon, either, because they were too busy arguing.

"Why do I always have to be in the back row?"

"Stop stepping on my feet!"

"How come her pom-poms are bigger than my pom-poms?"

"Why do I have to be stuck next to *her*?"

"Listen up!" Faybelle stepped onto a bench and stood with her hands on her hips. "As head cheer-hexer, I'm calling an emergency meeting."

"Emergency?" The girls dropped their pom-poms.

Duchess cocked her head, trying to catch every word, but the closest flamingo had started snoring. As gracefully as possible, so as not to attract attention, Duchess moved to a spot next to a different flamingo. The cheerhexers remained focused on their leader.

"Did you see that pathetic display in the Castle-teria?" Faybelle asked. Her wings twitched. "*I'm* the only student in General Villainy who deserves the A grade and the title of Next Top Villain. Sparrow doesn't care. Ginger's too sugary sweet. Lizzie can't even fake a temper tantrum. Duchess doesn't have a single drop of evil in her bloodline, and Raven…" She paused. Then her face flushed red, and her wings stiffened. "Raven Queen is single-handedly ruining the reputations of evildoers everywhere! What's her problem? Who wouldn't want to be evil? *Who?*"

One of the cheerhexers started to raise her hand, but after a sharp glance from Faybelle, she dropped her arm to her side and stepped to the back of the group.

Faybelle cleared her throat. Her wings relaxed. "As you know, I intend to become the vilest, meanest, wickedest Ever After High student ever," she said. "And I'm going to start my long evil career by acing this thronework assignment."

"What are you going to do?" one of the girls asked. "A magical cheer?"

"We're not supposed to do magical cheers," another said.

"They're forbidden. We'll get into trouble."

Faybelle flipped her long blond hair away from her face. "Oh, stop throwing pixie fits. *You're* not going to do a magical cheer. *I'm* going to do it because I have something up my sleeve." That appeared to be a literal statement because she reached up her sleeve. Then she pulled out a tiny black satchel.

The cheerhexers *ooh*ed. Duchess wobbled on her leg, almost losing her balance. Fairy dust! One of the most powerful magical ingredients in all the fairytale kingdoms. How could Duchess possibly sabotage a plan that contained fairy dust magic?

"What should I use it on?" Faybelle asked with an evil smile. The bag dangled from her outstretched arm. Each of the cheerhexers took two steps back. Then Faybelle laughed. "Relax. Why would I use it on you guys? You're my . . . *BFFAs*."

They all giggled nervously. But no one looked convinced. Most of the girls grabbed their pom-poms and flew off the field.

Faybelle looked around. Then her gaze rested on the hedgehogs' pen. "Hmmm." She flew off the bench and landed in front of the little fence that protected Lizzie's precious living croquet balls. She knelt and peered through the wires. The little critters were also taking naps, curled into spiky balls. "Well, well, what have we here?" Faybelle asked.

Duchess's heart started to pound. Faybelle wouldn't hurt the hedgehogs, would she? No one could be that evil. Could they?

Only one cheerhexer remained. "What are you going to do?" she asked.

"I'm going to get an A on my thronework assignment, that's what."

Faybelle walked over to the hedgehogs' trough and performed a quiet cheer. "Faybelle, Faybelle, she's the one. She's the one who'll make hedgehogs fun." She opened her satchel and sprinkled some of the fairy dust into her hand. The dust sparkled like stars. That was when Duchess realized that the cheer had been a magical incantation. The other cheerhexer watched as Faybelle leaned over the fence and stretched out her hand. "I've always wondered why they're called hedge*hogs*." Glittery flecks of magic drifted down, landing in the trough. Faybelle tucked the satchel back up her sleeve, a smile spreading across her face. "Don't wake them up yet," she said. "I want Mr. Badwolf to witness the transformation. Won't Lizzie Hearts be surprised when she finds that her sweet little babies are real hogs!"

Faybelle's wings unfurled, and she flew toward the school. The other cheerhexer followed.

There was no time to transform. Duchess squeezed between flamingos and flew over the fence. Then she landed in the hedgehog pen. The little critters opened their eyes and yawned. They stretched their little legs. Duchess had disturbed their naptime, and soon they'd head for the trough, because if there was one thing a hedgehog liked better than napping, it was eating!

How shocking it would be for Lizzie to find her pen filled with hogs. And how disappointing it would be if Faybelle got the A.

Duchess reached her wing into the trough. The plan, formed at that very moment, was to scoop out the enchanted hedgehog kibble and get rid of it. But wings don't work in the same way that hands work. She groaned and glanced over at the school. Faybelle was already inside. It wouldn't be long before she found Mr. Badwolf and persuaded him to follow her back to the pen.

Duchess hissed at the hedgehogs as they waddled toward their lunch. They squealed and curled back into balls. She didn't like scaring them, but it was definitely better than being turned into real hogs. Duchess reached her long neck into the trough, then groaned. She thought she'd be able to peck out the glittery flakes, but they had camouflaged themselves among the hedgehogs' food. And so, as quickly as possible, she pecked the kibble, until it was all gone and her beak was full. Then she flew over the fence and spat the kibble into a garbage can.

I did it, she thought. The trough was empty, and all the hedgehogs were still small, fat, and spiky. They were not happy, however, because they still expected their post-nap meal. Their noses sniffing, they moseyed up to the empty trough and climbed in. Grunts of dissatisfaction filled the air.

But Duchess was so happy about the outcome that she wanted to do a cheer. She twirled on her webbed feet. The flamingos looked at her as if she were crazy. She'd foiled a fairy! The A was almost hers.

By the time Duchess had ducked behind an equipment shed and had transformed back into her human self, Mr. Badwolf was following Faybelle toward the hedgehog pen. Blondie was there, too, her MirrorPad in hand. The cheerhexers and a few snoopy students were close behind.

Everyone was breathless by the time they reached the pen. Duchess peered around the edge of the shed, careful to stay out of sight.

"Why are we out here?" Mr. Badwolf asked. He tucked his tie beneath his vest and smoothed his jacket. "I have no interest in croquet."

"We're out here because I've done my thronework assignment," Faybelle announced. She whistled. "Wake up, little croquet balls. Wake up and eat your lunch."

"They're already awake," Blondie said, pointing into the trough.

"Oh, so they are." Faybelle nudged Mr. Badwolf with her elbow. "You're going to be sooooo impressed."

"I will be the judge of that, Ms. Thorn," he growled.

Everyone looked in the trough. The hedgehogs sat on their round behinds, their arms folded, their tummies rumbling.

Faybelle leaned over the fence. "What the hex? The food is gone, so how come they haven't changed?"

Mr. Badwolf tapped his clipboard against his leg. "Ms. Thorn? What is the meaning of this?"

"I used fairy dust," she explained. "I sprinkled it in their food. Fairy dust never fails. Never!" Her voice rose an octave and cracked.

"Fairy *dust* might not fail, but fairies do," Mr. Badwolf said. He removed his red pen from his vest pocket. "You get an FF on your assignment, Ms. Thorn."

Faybelle balled her hands into fists. Her wings beat furiously. "Someone ruined my thronework!"

Duchess slipped away as quickly and quietly as possible, holding her laugh until she was sure Faybelle couldn't hear her.

A House of Cards

By Wednesday evening, Duchess was exhausted. After sabotaging both Ginger's and Faybelle's General Villainy thronework, she'd attended her lesson at the Red Shoes Studio and her Home Economyths class. She wanted to fall into bed, but a letter was waiting for her on her desk. She immediately recognized the handwriting.

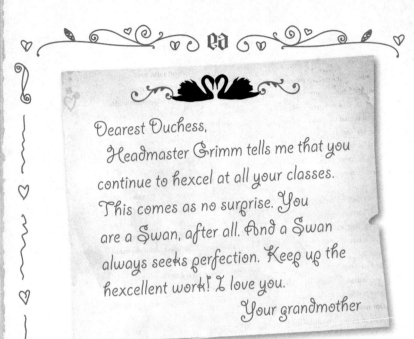

Dearest Duchess,

Headmaster Grimm tells me that you continue to hexcel at all your classes. This comes as no surprise. You are a Swan, after all. And a Swan always seeks perfection. Keep up the hexcellent work! I love you.

Your grandmother

Duchess gazed out the window, toward the distant land where her family's palace stood. *Will you still love me when you learn that I want to change my destiny?*

"Did you hear what she said about me?" Lizzie asked as she barreled into the room. "Oh, she makes my blood boil!"

Duchess tucked the letter into her drawer. "Who makes your blood boil?"

"That Blondie Lockes and her gossipy MirrorCast. I'm not quitting. I'm totally capable of doing both

thronework assignments. I'm…ouch!" She rubbed her bottom.

"What's the matter?" Duchess asked.

"I'm so sore," Lizzie moaned. "I've been practicing my equestrian skills all day. But my horse and I got into a big fight. When I ordered it to go left, it went right. And when I ordered it to stop, it kept on going. So I gave it a time-out, but it nipped me. And Blondie was there and she saw the whole thing. You're so lucky you don't have to practice."

Duchess smiled sympathetically. "I've been riding my whole life. It must be hard to start learning so late."

"I wouldn't have to ride a horse if this school were in Wonderland. My playing-card army would carry me wherever I wanted to go!" Lizzie marched into the closet, where she took off her riding clothes and put on her pajamas, a cute matching set with red hearts. Duchess was so tired she could have slept in her clothes. But there was another matter to attend to.

"Lizzie?" she asked, trying to keep her voice steady and not give away her evil intentions. "You seem totally

stressed out. Why not focus on the Princessology thronework and forget about the General Villainy thronework?" If Lizzie quit, it would certainly make Duchess's task easier. One fewer villain to sabotage, and she wouldn't have to double-cross her roommate.

Lizzie pulled her wild hair into a ponytail. "You think I should quit?" She frowned.

Duchess tried to look sympathetic. "It might make you feel better."

Just then, both of their MirrorPhones chimed. It was a hext from Blondie:

Be sure to watch JUST RIGHT tomorrow to see if Lizzie quits under pressure.

Lizzie tossed her phone onto her bed. "That Blondie thinks she's so much better than me, just because she has that stupid show. Well, I'm the daughter of a *real* queen. She's the daughter of some girl who scared a bunch of bears." Lizzie's cheeks turned as red as the hearts on her pajamas. "She wants a scoop? I'll give her a scoop. I'm gonna go all Evil Queen on her. Just

you wait and see." She pulled a card out of her magic deck. Her mother, the Queen of Hearts, had written inspirational messages on them, and Lizzie often consulted her mother's advice in times of crisis. "'Look, a book is a terrible thing to taste,'" Lizzie read out loud.

"What does that mean?" asked Duchess.

Lizzie marched over to her bookcase. "It means the Princess of Hearts isn't going to quit!"

"What are you doing?" Duchess asked.

"I'm doing my General Villainy thronework, that's what I'm doing." She grabbed a book. "I'll teach Blondie a lesson, Wonderland-style."

Drat! It would have been so much easier if she'd quit. But the good news was, Duchess wouldn't have to change into her swan form to eavesdrop. "What's your plan?" she asked.

"You know how Mr. Badwolf told us to look to our family stories for inspiration? Well, that's exactly what I'm going to do." Lizzie sat on her bed. Duchess sat next to her. "Have you ever read this?" Lizzie asked as she opened the book to its title page.

"I remember my grandmother reading it to me," Duchess said.

Shuffle, the hedgehog, crawled out from under the covers and sat on Lizzie's lap while she flipped through the pages. There was a drawing of a girl named Alice who was wearing an apron. There was another drawing of Alice with a neck as long as a telescope. Lizzie pointed and giggled. "That looks pretty rotten and nasty to me."

"You're going to stretch her into a giant?" Duchess asked. "But you don't have the power to do that."

"Oh, relax. I'm not going to enlarge her," Lizzie said. "Can you imagine? She's loud enough in her *normal* size." Lizzie pointed to the text. "But look, Alice got so big she couldn't fit through the garden door. She was trapped! That's what I'm going to do. I'm going to trap Blondie. She won't be able to move. And she won't be able to do her MirrorCast!"

She pushed the book aside and set Shuffle on the

 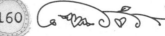

plush gold carpet. Then Lizzie grabbed her deck of cards and, with a practiced flick of her wrist, the cards flew into the air.

The filigreed cards soared overhead, then fell around Shuffle. The hedgehog squeaked as the cards formed a little log cabin. Shuffle's snout wiggled as it stuck out the window. There was no room for her to turn around, and no door from which to escape.

Lizzie smiled at her accomplishment.

Duchess crouched next to the card house. "Wow. Your mom would be really proud." Lizzie was showing signs of villainous potential. If she carried out this plan, she'd surely get the A.

"Of course, I'll only entrap Blondie for a little while," Lizzie explained. "I mean, she needs to eat, right? And what if her legs start to cramp?"

Okay, maybe not very villainous.

"This will teach Blondie a lesson. Don't mess with the heart of Wonderland!" Lizzie snapped her fingers, and the cards flew back into their box. Shuffle waddled off.

Lizzie tucked her deck under her pillow, then climbed into bed. "Do you know what you're going to do?" she asked Duchess.

"No," Duchess lied.

"You'll figure something out." Lizzie yawned and rolled over. "You always get the best grades. Well, good night."

It was only a few moments before the snoring began. Duchess was used to the sound. There'd been many a night when Duchess had lain awake, staring at the ceiling, worrying about her schoolwork and her destiny, while Lizzie had been in a deep sleep. Even with the worries of Wonderland, Lizzie didn't seem to know the meaning of insomnia.

Once Lizzie's snoring had fallen into a rhythmic pattern, Duchess tiptoed out of the room. She knew exactly what had to be done in order to sabotage Lizzie's plans. It would have been nice, though, to see Blondie trapped in a card house. Maybe another time.

Since most everyone was settling into bed, the

dormitory's Common Room was quiet and dark. Duchess hurried to the corner shelves, which were cluttered with all sorts of board games like Babble, Charm-opoly, and Toil and Trouble. She squinted into the darkness, searching for the small boxes of Ever After High playing cards. Finding one, she grabbed it. The cards inside wouldn't match Lizzie's, but it was the best she could do at this late hour.

Duchess turned to go back to her room when she tripped on something. "Oops," she said as she stumbled forward. She was about to do a face-plant when two hands clutched her waist and whisked her back onto her feet.

"Thank you," she said, her eyes straining in the darkness. Who had caught her?

"You're welcome." For an instant, a blinding light illuminated the room, then disappeared.

Prince Daring Charming's smile was better than a flashlight.

Broken Hearts

uchess was so startled that she honked!

Because the Common Room was bathed in evening silence, Duchess's honk sounded louder than it usually did. She was mortified. It was bad enough that she'd honked in front of the prince of her dreams, but if she wasn't able to change her destiny, then she'd be making that sound for the rest of her life.

"Sorry," she told him. "I didn't mean to fall on you."

"No need to apologize for fainting," he said as he

sat in a leather chair. "I'm used to it. It's one of the many effects I have on girls."

"Uh, I didn't faint. I tripped on something." She looked down. His sword lay on the carpet. Then she noticed he was wearing pajamas that were embroidered with the Charming family crest. A dragon-shaped pillow was tucked under his arm. "Are you sleeping out here?"

"I was trying to," he said. "All that serenading under my window makes it hard to sleep, so I came here to find some peace and quiet. Don't get me wrong—I love the adoration, but even a perfect prince needs rest."

And needs a perfect princess, she thought.

She stood there, staring at his handsomeness. His jawline was so strong it looked as if it had been chiseled from granite. The straightness of his nose was indisputable. And his locks were so thick and wavy a cricket could surf on them!

"You play?" he asked, his gaze falling on the card deck in her hand.

"No," she said, momentarily forgetting why she'd come to the Common Room.

"Then why are you holding that deck?"

Oops. "Um, well, Lizzie loves cards." She immediately regretted mentioning her roommate's name, because Daring's eyes got really wide and he took a deep breath.

"You know Lizzie?"

"Yeah, I'm her roommate." *Feather dusters!* Would this guy ever remember who she was? Would she have to always reintroduce herself?

"You room with Lizzie?" He darted to his feet. "Then can you explain something to me? I offered Lizzie the opportunity to accompany me on a stroll, but I fear she did not understand the situation. You see, there is currently a waiting list for this privilege, but I am willing to scoot her to the front of the line. Clearly, she only needs to be informed of this fact, and then she will accept my invitation."

Duchess frowned. Was Daring that dense? Was it impossible for him to believe that a girl didn't want

to date him? "I don't think Lizzie's interested," she said gently.

"Not interested?" He looked completely baffled. If this was his biggest conundrum, then he truly lived a charmed life. "But..."

Was Duchess supposed to give him relationship advice? *Hello? What about me?*

"I could take a stroll with you," she said with a wave of courage.

"The waiting list is hanging on my door. Feel free to add your name." Then he sank onto the chair and sighed, as if his heart were breaking.

Duchess squeezed the card deck, her face flushing. Was she angrier at Lizzie for stealing Daring's heart or at Daring for not noticing her own heart? No way would she ever add her name to a waiting list. After she was declared Next Top Villain and she graduated to Advanced Villainy, she'd learn how to make a love potion and she'd spray it all over him, and when he fell in love with her, she'd tell him to put *his* name on a waiting list!

No longer caring if she was heard, Duchess stomped out of the Common Room.

Lizzie was still snoring. Pirouette had returned and was settled in her nest. Duchess crossed the room, careful to step over the messy piles of clothing and shoes. Then she stood beside Lizzie's bed. Luckily, Lizzie had rolled away from the pillow and was sleeping sideways. Carefully, Duchess reached under the pillow, where Lizzie had stashed her Wonderland deck. Immediate pain shot through her finger. She pulled out her hand to find two little tooth marks and two drops of blood.

Shuffle!

Duchess pushed the pillow aside. The hedgehog was lying on top of the card deck. "Give me that," she whispered. Shuffle glared at her. Then the critter wrapped her arms around the deck. A little tug-of-war ensued. "In case you hadn't noticed, I'm bigger than you." After a few shakes, Shuffle flew across the room and landed with a soft plop in a pile of towels.

Her finger throbbing, Duchess opened the Wonderland box and removed the deck of cards. Then she slid the school deck into the box. Lizzie was always in such a hurry in the morning, she never took the time to look inside the box. Why would she? No one had ever replaced her cards.

After tucking the Wonderland box back under the pillow, Duchess hid the real deck in Lizzie's desk, to make it look as if Lizzie had misplaced it. Lizzie would eventually find it, just not tomorrow morning. The deed was done.

After bandaging her finger, Duchess stood at the open window. Tomorrow, Lizzie would be out. She'd be embarrassed when her card trick didn't work. She'd be furious when she discovered that her own roommate and friend had double-crossed her. But even with a fairy-fail on her record, Lizzie Hearts would still inherit a kingdom, or at least live her life playing croquet and drinking tea on two human legs. So maybe she'd understand Duchess's motives.

Maybe.

A dim light drew Duchess's attention. She leaned outside. With Ginger, Faybelle, Sparrow, and Lizzie eliminated, only one competitor remained. And her light was still on.

It was time to see what Raven was planning.

Raven's Room

*D*uchess tucked her wings, then perched on the dormitory's stone ledge. As gracefully as possible, which is difficult when one has webbed feet, she stepped close to the window and peered through.

Raven's desk lamp glowed. Her side of the room was a tangle of thorny branches and dark oak furniture. The ambience was foreboding. The decor had been chosen by Raven's roommate, Apple White, to fit the image of what Raven was expected to be. The future Evil Queen was not supposed to surround herself with ruffles and colors, like Apple's side of the room.

Raven sat slumped over her desk, writing. She was dressed in black leggings and an embellished hoodie, her purple-highlighted hair tied back from her face. Her expression was serious. Was she working on a to-do list, or writing in her diary? Maybe she was working on the thronework assignment.

"Did you read the hext from Blondie?" Apple asked as she flitted past the desk, her long nightgown drowning in ruffles. Luckily, the window was cracked open, so Duchess had no trouble eavesdropping.

"No."

"She said that Lizzie Hearts might quit the Next Top Villain contest."

"So?"

"So?" Apple squeaked. "You should be happy to hear that news. If Lizzie quits, it will make it easier for you to win." She stood in front of her magic mirror, brushing her hair. "You're going to win, right?"

"I don't know."

"You don't know?" Apple whipped around. "But you must win. You're destined to be my Evil Queen."

"What-ever-after," Raven grumbled. "Look, I'm trying to read."

Apple's eyes widened. "What are you reading? Is it for your General Villainy thronework? What are you going to do? Will it be scary? Am I going to be the victim, which I'm totally willing to do, by the way? Should I alert the dwarves?"

Duchess leaned closer, pressing her beak to the glass. This was it. Raven was going to tell Apple about her rotten and nasty plan. A shiver of anticipation ran through Duchess's feathers.

But Raven didn't say anything. She turned the page, then glanced up at the window. Her eyes flashed. *Oops.* Duchess pulled her long neck away from the glass. *Did she see me?*

Raven didn't come to the window, so it appeared that Duchess was in the clear.

"Well, whatever spell you decide to cast, I know it

will be the best. I mean, the rottenest." Apple giggled. "No one else can be the Next Top Villain but you, Raven. And then our destinies will begin, and you'll become the evilest in our kingdoms and you'll feed me that poisoned apple, and I'll fall asleep and be kissed by Daring Charming, and live Happily Ever After, and it will be royally enchanting!"

Hate to tell you this, Duchess thought, *but when I get named Next Top Villain, Daring won't be able to take his eyes off* me.

"I think you should stop worrying so much about our destinies," Raven said. "Sometimes it's better to live in the moment and not for the future."

Easy for you to say, Duchess thought.

She shifted her weight on the ledge. Still hidden from sight, she cocked her head, listening for more conversation.

Apple hummed a little song, then said, "I'm going to bed now. Charm you later."

"Good night," Raven said drily.

Wow, talk about the odd couple. Duchess thought

that she and Lizzie were the most mismatched pair in the dorm, but these two were like sugar and salt.

Suddenly, the window slid open and Raven stuck out her head. "Hello, Duchess," she said.

Duchess honked.

"Are you spying on me?" She rested her chin in her hand. "Trying to find out what I'm doing for General Villainy?"

Duchess blinked.

"I know it's you. You want me to think you're Pirouette, but I can tell it's you. Want to know how?"

As far as Duchess knew, she and Pirouette looked identical. No one had ever been able to tell them apart. She tore a piece of ivy off the wall and began to eat it, pretending she hadn't understood a word.

"I can tell it's you because you stand like a ballerina." She pointed to Duchess's webbed feet.

True enough, Duchess's feet were turned out in first position.

Flustered, Duchess flew away.

Revealed

uring breakfast in the Castleteria the next morning, Sparrow Hood joined Duchess and Lizzie at their table. Lizzie had purposefully selected one in the center of the room so her brilliant Villainy thronework scheme could be witnessed by all.

Sparrow set his guitar on the table, then smiled mischievously at Duchess. "What's up, Swan?" He grabbed a piece of toast from her plate. "Anything *new*?"

Duchess didn't reply. She was staring at the nearest mirror. Photos of the six General Villainy

students were posted on the screen, three with gold
X's over their faces.

Only Raven, Lizzie, and Duchess remained, and
soon, it would be just her and Raven. During last
night's overheard conversation, Raven hadn't seemed
very enthusiastic about the General Villainy thronework, which was good news for Duchess. The A
could still be hers to claim.

"Whoa!" Sparrow pushed his guitar aside, nar-
rowly avoiding a splash of hot tea. The teacup in
Lizzie's hand was rattling on its saucer because she
was trembling. "What's your problem, Hearts?"

Lizzie had been a nervous wreck all morning.
"Mind your own rabbit hole!"

"You're in a rotten mood," Sparrow said. "Hey,
you're not planning something rotten and nasty,
are you? I heard you were going to quit."

"That's a big, fat fable." Lizzie clenched her jaw. "I'm not telling you anything, and don't bother talking to Duchess. She won't tell you a thing, because roommates do not squeal on each other." Lizzie set her cup on the table. "Now, I order you to go away. You're blocking my view."

"View of what?" He looked around. "Are you drooling over Charming like all the other girls?" Daring sat two tables away, surrounded by his groupies. "What about me? I'm drool-worthy."

"I don't care about Daring Charming." She rolled up her sleeves, preparing for the big surprise. "Listen, stop bothering me. I have a lot on my mind, and I need to pay attention."

Fortunately for Duchess, Lizzie had been in such a hurry that she'd grabbed the card deck and had shoved it into her pocket without looking inside. There was a very strong possibility that Duchess's sabotage would work, and Lizzie would soon be out of the contest.

That realization made Duchess's stomach clench. Did evil villains feel guilt? She doubted it.

Sparrow scooted closer to Duchess. "So, if your roommate is going to do something rotten and nasty, should I take cover?" He winked at Duchess. Fortunately, Lizzie did not notice the wink.

She was on the lookout for one person. "Oh, there she is," Lizzie said with a gasp.

Blondie Lockes hurried into the Castleteria, MirrorPad in hand. She spun left, then right, always on the lookout for a scoop. Spying Lizzie, she headed straight for the table. "So, are you going to quit?" she asked. She didn't even bother with a "good morning."

"To quit or not to quit? That is the question," Sparrow said, stealing another piece of Duchess's toast.

Lizzie opened her mouth, but Blondie didn't wait for the answer. "I conducted an official poll," Blondie said. "Well, maybe not *official*. I asked a bunch of people, and most of them think you're going to quit because there's no way you can compete with Raven." Blondie pressed the RECORD button on her MirrorPad. "Are you going to quit?"

Lizzie growled. Then she leaped to her feet, almost knocking over her breakfast teapot. Duchess had seen Lizzie throw a fit before, but she'd never seen her like this. Her fists were clenched, and her face turned so red it looked as if it had been painted. "You want to know if I'm going to quit?" she asked as she climbed onto the table. "You want to know if I'm going to *quit*?"

The Castleteria went silent as everyone turned to watch the spectacle that was unfolding in the center of the room. Raven looked up from her book and raised her eyebrows. For a moment, the only sound was Lizzie's crazed breathing. Lizzie reached into her pocket and pulled out the box of cards. This was it. Duchess felt a little queasy with anticipation. Blondie was being such a pain, and she totally deserved to be trapped in a card house for the whole day. In fact, she deserved way worse than that. But Lizzie's revenge wouldn't happen. The cards had no magic. This was going to be so embarrassing for Lizzie. Duchess wanted to run from the room. She couldn't face what she'd done.

Lizzie opened the card box. "A Heart might twitter, a Heart might flitter, but the Princess of Hearts is never a quitter! Prepare yourself for something rotten and nasty." She tossed her cards at Blondie. Everyone gasped.

The cards flew through the air. Lizzie beamed with happiness, believing her revenge to be close at hand. Duchess cringed.

The cards fell at Blondie's feet. No one moved. Somewhere in the Castleteria, a cricket chirped.

Lizzie stood on the table, her mouth open with surprise. "Holy rabbit hole!" She pointed at the scattered cards. "Those aren't mine."

Mr. Badwolf strode over to the table. His coffee mug had the words WORLD'S BADDEST DAD printed on the side. "Throwing cards at someone is neither rotten nor nasty." He looked up at her. "You didn't

even give your intended victim a paper cut. I'm very disappointed." He waved his clipboard. "Fairy-fail for you, Ms. Hearts."

Blondie typed something onto her MirrorPad, and a big gold X appeared over Lizzie's photo on all the mirrors.

Lizzie jumped off the table and picked up one of the cards, staring at it with confusion. "How did these ordinary cards get into my Wonderland box? I demand an answer!"

Sparrow gave Duchess a conspiratorial look. Duchess stepped close to Lizzie and spoke quietly to her. "I wouldn't worry about it," she said. "What's done is done. Now you can focus on the Princess-ology thronework. That's more important to you, right?" Hopefully, Lizzie would see this as no big deal.

But that's when Daring Charming stepped forward. With a grand sweep of his arm, he bowed before Lizzie. Then, standing as straight as a tree, he cleared his throat and said, "It is my duty, as the hero, to come to the damsel's rescue." He pointed at

Duchess. "That girl took a deck of cards from the Common Room last night."

That girl? Duchess grimaced. Would he ever remember her name? It was bad enough that he didn't pay any attention to her and was crushing on someone else, but now he was ratting on her.

She was beginning to suspect that their love was not meant to be.

"Duchess?" Lizzie turned, her eyes wide with disbelief. "What's he talking about?"

Duchess wasn't sure what to do. Her instinct was to deny everything and try to save her friendship with Lizzie. So what if she took a deck of cards? That was circumstantial evidence, right? There were no eyewitnesses to the actual crime, except for a hedgehog, and she was sleeping back in the dorm room.

On the other hand, if Duchess denied doing the deed, then she wouldn't get credit for it when Mr. Badwolf assigned the grade.

Dilemma drama.

"Did you switch my cards?" Lizzie asked, her

voice cracking with emotion. "Did you ruin my thronework?"

Everyone was waiting for the answer. Everyone was staring at her, except for Sparrow, who already knew the answer. He was eating the last of her toast. Duchess stood so stiffly she felt like a statue. What should she say? She wanted to transform and fly away.

"Wait a sweet second," Ginger Breadhouse said. She pushed her way between Daring and Lizzie. Her felt jacket was decorated with white swirls, like icing. "Now that I think about it, Duchess was in the Cooking Class-ic Room. I thought she was there because she'd smelled my delicious cinnamon trolls, but now I'm thinking she was there to mess up my plan." Ginger put her hands on her hips. "That's why my sandman powder didn't work. She ruined it!"

Then Faybelle Thorn flew forward. "Someone ruined my fairy dust spell. But look what that *someone* left behind." She held up a white feather.

Faybelle, Ginger, and Lizzie glared at Duchess. She

took a long, deep breath, trying to keep herself calm. Her scheme wasn't supposed to be revealed yet. She still had to learn what Raven was planning and ruin it. But now Raven would know what she was up to. "I…I…" Duchess swallowed hard. "I really don't know what you're all talking about."

Mr. Badwolf set his coffee cup on the table and began to write on his clipboard. "Sabotaging your competitors, Ms. Swan? That is most promising. However, I must get one thing clear." He pointed his red pen at her. "Were your intentions to eliminate the other students? In that case, I would be pleased. Or were your intentions to save the rest of the student body from the effects of rotten and nasty plans? In that case, I would be *displeased*."

If she denied her intentions, he'd give her a fairy-fail. There was nothing she could do. "I wanted to win," Duchess admitted.

Mr. Badwolf growled happily. Lizzie's eyes filled with tears. "How could you? I thought you were my friend." She grabbed her book bag and ran off.

"Lizzie, wait!" Duchess called. She wanted to explain. But Lizzie was gone, her sobs fading. An ache filled Duchess's heart, but only for a moment. She held her head high. So what if she didn't have a friend? She was a ballerina, and solitude was not her enemy.

Mr. Badwolf patted her on the shoulder. "Sabotaging your competitors was a good start, Ms. Swan. But double-crossing someone *and* making her cry is even better." He tucked the clipboard under his arm. "I will wait to assign your grade until I've seen what Ms. Queen has up her wicked sleeves."

"You don't have to wait!" a voice announced.

It was Raven Queen, and she stood on a table on the far side of the Castleteria. Her arms were held wide. What was she doing? "Now it's my turn!"

Some of the students screamed. Except for Apple White, who was bouncing on her toes. "I knew she'd do it. I knew she'd be bad!"

Students rushed toward the exits. The cooks hid behind their cauldrons. Those with fairy wings flew

into the rafters. The daughter of the Evil Queen was about to unleash her thronework assignment!

Duchess should have been scared, but instead, she was frustrated. All her efforts were about to be ruined by Raven's sorcery. Duchess would fail General Villainy. She'd fail at being a Rebel. And she'd lose her only friend in the process.

Raven raised her arms higher and higher, and a spell emerged from her mouth.

Raven's

Ruse

*R*aven Queen looked like the perfect villain. Her long black hair whipped around her as if caught in a storm. The spell was spoken. She flicked her outstretched fingers.

Blam!

A black cloud of smoke appeared on the table in front of her. This was it. Rotten and nasty. Raven Queen would claim her place as the Next Top Villain.

Duchess held her breath, waiting to see what

emerged. Would it be a swarm of bees? A plague of locusts? Or maybe a knot of toads?

Honk!

The smoke faded away, and everyone started laughing. For what sat on the table, its legs splayed, was an ugly baby bird.

"What is *that*?" Raven asked, her hands on her hips.

"It's just a duck," Blondie said, disappointed.

"A duck?" Sparrow laughed. "Oooh, someone call security."

"It's not a duck," Duchess said. "It's a cygnet. A baby swan." The little thing looked confused. It started waddling around, honking like crazy. Duchess dashed across the room and grabbed it just before it fell off the table.

"How dare you!" Raven hollered, her eyes flaming. "Did you see that, Mr. Badwolf? Duchess sabotaged my thronework, just like she did to Ginger, Faybelle, and Lizzie."

What the hex? Duchess looked up at Raven, who still stood on the table.

"I don't know how you did it, Duchess, but you've totally ruined my plans." Raven folded her arms and pouted. "I'm really, really upset about this."

As Duchess cradled the cygnet in her arms, she tried to figure out what was going on. Had Raven's spell gone bad on its own? Or was it possible that Raven was...*trying* to lose?

"I guess that means I'm out of the contest," Raven said with a big shrug. "Oh well."

Blondie held her MirrorPad up to Mr. Badwolf's face. "Does this mean Raven Queen gets a fairy-fail on her thronework assignment? Is she out of the contest?"

"That's what it means," Raven said. She stepped off the table. "I congratulate you, Duchess. I guess you're the Next Top Villain."

"Nooooo!" Apple screeched. "This is not happening. Raven's supposed to be the Next Top Villain. My destiny depends on her." With her hand on her forehead, she fainted, landing right in Daring Charming's strong arms.

"Not so fast!" Mr. Badwolf roared. A wave of hot air blew across everyone's face. The cooks darted back behind their cauldrons. "I am most disappointed in you, Ms. Queen. Allowing yourself to be sabotaged is a rookie mistake. You should know better."

"Does that mean Duchess wins?" Blondie asked.

Mr. Badwolf grabbed his coffee cup. "I will announce the winner at the end of school Friday." Then he headed toward the teachers' lounge.

Duchess couldn't believe it. "Wait, what?" she asked, following him. "Why do we have to wait until Friday? I won, didn't I? I foiled everyone's plans, so that earns me the A."

"That remains to be seen, Ms. Swan."

She stopped walking. Her arms suddenly felt so heavy she almost dropped the baby swan. Angry tears stung her eyes. *That remains to be seen?* But she'd successfully completed the thronework, while everyone else had failed.

Sparrow grabbed his guitar. "Don't worry," he told her. "You totally rocked it. You've got the win, for sure."

Yes, she told herself. *I won*. But until Mr. Badwolf made the announcement, she had no A and no chance at a different destiny. The only thing she knew for sure was that she'd destroyed her friendship with Lizzie.

The room began to spin. She needed fresh air. She needed to fly. With the baby swan tucked in the crook of her arm, she hurried through the Castleteria and out into the courtyard.

Raven was just a few steps ahead. Duchess picked up her pace and caught up to her. "Why did you do that?" Duchess asked. "Why'd you pretend that I'd sabotaged your spell?"

Raven looked around. "Follow me. Quick, before Blondie sees us."

Duchess and Raven hurried down a steep staircase and into an alley behind the school. A sour scent filled Duchess's nostrils. This was where the garbage trucks came and went. Stacks of wooden crates lined a damp wall. Some bins of rotting vegetables were being attacked by the Pied Piper's rats.

It wasn't very pretty, which made it a great place to talk because none of the other Royals would be caught dead back there.

They stepped into the shadows behind a garbage container. The cygnet had fallen asleep, its little head tucked in the crook of Duchess's arm. "I know you don't like me," Raven said.

"I never—"

"Oh, please, don't bother denying it. You glare at me all the time. But I'm used to it. Lots of people don't like me. It comes with being the daughter of the most terrifying woman in fairytale history." She sighed. "But I feel I can trust you. You're not like the other Royals."

"What do you mean?" Duchess asked innocently. She wasn't ready to admit anything.

Raven tucked her black hair behind her ears. She looked right into Duchess's eyes and smiled knowingly. "You're different. You don't want your destiny."

"But…" Was it that obvious? Duchess had done

her best to hide her feelings from everyone. How could Raven know?

"Don't bother denying it. I don't want mine, either. In that way, we're the same."

A bin of rotten radishes overturned as a rat scurried away. Duchess didn't startle or shriek. A hundred rats could have held a parade in that alley, and she wouldn't have cared. All she knew, at that moment, was that the daughter of the Evil Queen knew exactly how she felt.

"I get that you want the perfect grades, Duchess. I also get that you'd like to win Next Top Villain so you can go on to Advanced Villainy and learn dark magic."

Duchess nodded slowly.

"If it were up to me, everyone would have the right to change his or her destiny. So I wish you luck. But I think you should know that it won't be easy. If you want approval, then don't be a Rebel." She started to walk up the alley.

"Wait," Duchess called, catching up with her.

"Why don't you want your destiny? You could have everything. You could do anything you want."

Sadness filled Raven's eyes. "When you're a villain, people pretend to love you because they're afraid. And they despise you for the same reason." She reached out and ran her hand gently over the cygnet's downy back. "I never want anyone to be afraid of me." She turned and walked away, her black cape flowing with each heavy step.

The competition was over. Raven had purposefully failed the thronework. Everyone else was out. Mr. Badwolf would have no other choice but to declare Duchess the winner. At least, that was what she hoped. She should have felt ecstatic. But instead, she felt very alone.

She carried the cygnet to the pond and left it with the other swans. A female quickly adopted it, wrapping her wing protectively around its little body.

Duchess wished someone would wrap a wing around her.

Horsing

Around

It was a terribly long night. Lizzie didn't speak a word to Duchess. In fact, she built a wall out of cards, separating the sides of the room. There was lots of tossing and turning by both roommates, neither of them able to sleep. Even Pirouette seemed ruffled by the tension. She sat in her nest, preening excessively.

But now it was Friday morning. Mr. Badwolf's announcement would be made at the end of the day. Duchess would get the grade and the title. And

Sparrow would get to pick a prize from the treasure vault. These were the positive thoughts that Duchess replayed in her mind as she got dressed in her riding gear.

Lizzie refused to walk with her to their Princessology class. Even Shuffle gave her the cold, prickly shoulder. Whispers filled the hall. Students were looking at her differently. Was it respect for her accomplishments, or was it judgment? What did she care? Soon she'd be the prima ballerina. She shot a glare at Daring Charming. *Soon you won't need to be reminded of my name!* Her head held high, her chin out, she walked past all the gawkers. *I don't need any of you. I'm going to change my destiny, and you can't stop me.* Maybe Headmaster Grimm was right. Maybe she had a black swan side after all.

After grabbing a quick bite at the Castleteria, she looked around for Sparrow but didn't find him. Raven's picture had a big gold X over it, but there was no title beneath Duchess's picture. *Soon,* she told herself.

By the time she reached the stable, the other princesses were mounted and ready. Each had color-coordinated their riding attire to match their saddles and bridles. Manes had been braided, curled, and beaded. Hooves had been polished and painted. Lizzie had stenciled red hearts all over her horse. Raven's wore a black tiara.

"Excellent accessorizing," Mrs. Her Majesty the White Queen said as she made her rounds. "Magnificent mani-curses. Stupendous styling." Then she came to a dead stop at Duchess's horse. Duchess had been so busy with her General Villainy throne-work, and so worried about her friendship with Lizzie, she'd forgotten about appearances. "Going au naturel?" Mrs. Her Majesty asked with a curled lip. "A princess should never be seen on a plain horse. I do hope your riding skills make up for this unfortunate lapse."

"They will," Duchess assured her as she settled onto the saddle.

Blondie rode up to her. "Do you want to say anything to the viewers?"

"No."

"What about to Lizzie? Do you want to publicly apologize?"

Pretending not to hear the question, Duchess grabbed the reins and nudged her horse out of the stable.

The grandstand was full. Usually, no one would care about a Princessology thronework assignment. But thanks to Blondie Lockes and her *Just Right* MirrorCast, the drama between Lizzie and Duchess was all anyone was talking about. Even the teachers were in attendance, including Mr. Badwolf. As Duchess rode past, she caught bits of student conversation. "I hope Duchess fairy-fails. She deserves it for what she did to Lizzie." There were some *boos* directed at her. And lots of glaring.

If you want approval, then don't be a Rebel.

When Lizzie rode past the grandstand, Daring stood and cheered. The other princesses rode in a protective clump around her. "If Duchess fails, it will be sweet revenge for Lizzie," someone said.

Duchess knew she wouldn't fail. She was the best rider among them. She could ride with her eyes closed.

She was the first to take the course. The happy villagers, the angry villagers, the troll bridge, the dragon poop, the rainstorm, windstorm, and fairy hail—nothing forced her horse from the golden path. Duchess finished in record time. Mrs. Her Majesty greeted her at the end of the course and congratulated her with a perfect score.

Ashlynn, Briar, Apple, and the others took their turns. Despite a few setbacks—Ashlynn stopped to converse with a chipmunk, and Briar fell asleep on the troll bridge—they each made it to the end of the course. Then the princesses dismounted and gathered to watch the final rider. Duchess stood off to the side, alone.

Lizzie looked pretty in her gear. She'd tied a bright red sash around her waist. But she was visibly nervous, her riding crop shaking. She waved at the grandstand. Daring cheered her on. Then, her teeth clenched, her hands gripping the reins, she kicked her horse. It didn't budge. She kicked it again. It ate some grass. "I order you to *go!*" she hollered. After reaching back and nipping Lizzie's boot, the equally temperamental horse began to walk down the path.

Blondie sashayed over, her curly locks bouncing even after she'd come to a stop next to Duchess. "How does it feel to be a terrible roommate?" she whispered. "Do you feel bad about what you did?"

"No comment." Duchess pushed the MirrorPad away.

Then she turned toward the forest. She didn't want to see Lizzie fail the test. Two failures in as many days would be so humiliating. But there was no way to help her at this point. Lizzie would either keep to the golden path or she wouldn't. Gasps arose from the grandstand, but no screams, which meant Lizzie was managing to stay in the saddle. Maybe she'd make it. Duchess crossed her fingers.

But wait, what was that?

Sparrow Hood stood at the edge of the field, his green pants and hat blending perfectly into the forest backdrop. He set an amp on the ground, then slipped his guitar strap over his head. What was he doing? Was he going to play his guitar in the middle of Lizzie's test? Why would he do that? Didn't he remember that his muse-ic upset the horses?

Sparrow looked straight at her and smiled.

Duchess took a sharp breath. Of course he remembered.

The first chord shot out of the amp like an icicle to the brain. The second chord made her bones vibrate. As Sparrow launched into a frenzied string of chords, screaming arose from the grandstand.

Duchess whipped around. Lizzie's horse had gone into a wild rampage, its nostrils flared, its eyes wild. It charged right through a pile of dragon poop and headed for the troll bridge and the deep ravine.

"Help!" Lizzie cried. Her riding crop fell from her hand as she leaned forward to grip the horse's mane. If she was thrown into that ravine...

Daring Charming leaped from the grandstand. "I'll save you!" he called as he ran onto the obstacle course. But even though his legs were long and he was the best damsel-rescuer in the school, he would never be able to catch up to the horse, which was nearing the troll bridge at a full gallop. Mrs. Her Majesty the White Queen shouted for help into the receiver of an Emergency Prince Patrol phone. Blondie held her MirrorPad aloft, the record light glowing red. The other princesses watched with expressions of horror. Raven's face had gone paler than usual, and she stared helplessly at the unfolding chaos. Mr. Badwolf stood on one of the grandstand benches, straining to get a better view. Sparrow stopped playing. Tragedy was about to strike, and no one could get to Lizzie in time to stop it.

And then, just before the horse reached the bridge, the troll jumped out and blocked its path.

With a terrified whinny, the horse skidded to a stop. Lizzie lost her grip and was thrown into the air. She shrieked, her hands flailing as she reached out for something, for anything, that would stop her fall.

Duchess didn't try to hide the transformation. Before she'd even come up with a plan, she was in the air, soaring across the pasture, her wings beating as they'd never beat before. With a dancer's instinct and precision, she streamlined her body and flew at record speed. Lizzie began her descent, past the troll bridge and into the ravine. Every muscle in Duchess's body burned, but she pumped faster and faster until...

...she swooped into the ravine and grabbed Lizzie's red sash in her beak. But the weight was too much for Duchess's wings, and, together, the roommates began to plummet.

If Duchess Swan knew one thing, it was this: When she thought her body could take no more, she could always find a last reserve of strength. This was what ballet had taught her. All those endless

hours of training, of practicing a movement over and over until she thought she'd collapse. Then she'd dig deeper and find what she needed.

Her eyes closed, Duchess found what she needed, and she pumped those wings, until she gently lowered Lizzie onto the ground.

And then everything went black.

The End Is Just the Beginning

eyond the darkness, Lizzie's voice was saying, "She doesn't need a kiss to wake her up. Get out of the way!" Then she said, "Duchess? Can you hear me?"

Someone was gently shaking her.

When Duchess opened her eyes, the first thing she realized was that she was human again. Then she realized that Lizzie was okay, because Lizzie's smiling face was looking down at her.

Duchess turned her head to the right, then the

left. She was lying on the ground near the troll bridge. Mrs. Her Majesty the White Queen, Daring Charming, Raven, and the rest of the princesses had all gathered around. No one was glaring or booing.

"You saved me," Lizzie said. She started to kneel next to Duchess. Daring whipped off his letterman's jacket and placed it beneath Lizzie's knees.

"And I saved you from the mud," he announced with a flourish of his hand. "No need to thank me. Just doing my duty."

The mud was cold beneath Duchess's head, but Daring didn't bother offering her a jacket. Not even a sock. Even though she now realized that he wasn't one hundred percent perfect—because no one was, and that included herself—she still thought he was drop-dead gorgeous.

"I'd be as flat as a card if you hadn't swooped in and grabbed me," Lizzie said. "Thank you." She gave Duchess a hug.

Lizzie hugged her! Did this mean they were friends again?

Then Raven knelt beside her. "That was amazing. But I don't think the princes are very happy that you out-rescued them." Indeed, Daring and the members of the Emergency Prince Patrol were looking a bit red-faced. None of them made eye contact with Duchess.

A bell sounded in the distance, marking the end of the school day. Everyone turned to face the grandstand, where Mr. Badwolf stood, holding a megaphone. "It is time to announce the official grades for the General Villainy thronework," his voice boomed.

"And the winner of the Next Top Villain," Blondie hollered.

Lizzie and Raven helped Duchess to her feet. Her backside was coated in mud, but she didn't care. This was it. The moment she'd waited for.

Mr. Badwolf wiped spit from the corners of his mouth. "After reviewing the disappointing thronework from each of my students, I had decided that

Ms. Swan's acts of sabotage and double-crossing were worthy of an A grade."

Duchess smiled.

"But that has all changed." He snarled, revealing his canines. "Any villainy she practiced was erased by the fact that she rescued a princess. A villain *never* rescues a princess. That is unheard of. By being a do-gooder, Ms. Swan sabotaged her own grade. She receives a DG. So that means the A will be awarded to someone else."

Duchess's mouth fell open. The person walking across the grandstand, toward Mr. Badwolf, was Sparrow Hood.

"For disrupting the Princessology equestrian examination, and for forming an alliance with Ms. Swan and then double-crossing her, I hereby award Mr. Hood an A in General Villainy."

There were a few random claps, but no wild applause.

Duchess stared in shock as the grandstand's

mega-mirror lit up, and Sparrow's face filled the screen. A streaming headline read:

THIS JUST IN:
SPARROW HOOD WINS NEXT TOP VILLAIN

Blondie almost tripped on her own feet as she scrambled over the benches to get an interview. The obstacle course began to clear of people. The adoring and the angry villagers left, along with the troll. Students started heading back into the school, or down the lane toward Book End. Life returned to its normal fairytale pace.

Using Daring's jacket, Lizzie wiped mud from Duchess's face. "I don't care that I fairy-failed. I'm just glad that stupid Villainy thronework is over."

"It's only over until Badwolf gives us next week's Villainy thronework," Raven said.

Lizzie groaned.

Duchess felt light-headed, and her heart was beating quickly, like a bird's. It wasn't surprising that Sparrow had double-crossed her. She'd known he couldn't be trusted. But she'd surprised herself by failing. "I got a DG," she said quietly. "Do-gooder."

"Yep." Raven nodded. "And we got FF's. But at least Sparrow seems happy." They looked over at the grandstand. Sparrow beamed as he gave his interview, his proud smile almost as blinding as Daring's.

"He's happy because he'll get a prize from Badwolf's treasure vault," Duchess said. "At least he got what he wanted."

"But you didn't get what you wanted," Raven said.

No, she hadn't. She'd wanted to succeed so she could eventually change her destiny. But she hadn't changed anything…

…or had she?

Then Duchess realized something: Whether she called herself a Royal like Lizzie or a Rebel like Raven, one thing was perfectly clear. Standing on either side of her were two girls, each holding on to her arm, helping her across the field. She wasn't alone. Birds of a feather did flock together after all.

As they walked, a single feather drifted from Duchess's hair. It was the same size and shape as the other swan feathers that she found after transforming. Except for one thing.

It was black.

"That's random," Raven said as Duchess held the feather in her fingers.

"Not really," Lizzie pointed out. She pulled a card out of her deck and read the message her mother had written there. "*Without the black side of the chessboard, the white side would be fast asleep.* See?"

Duchess grinned. For the first time in her life, Riddlish made perfect sense. She was wide awake now, and she knew that whether she summoned her white swan side or her black swan side, her story, the one that belonged to her and to no one else, had yet to be written.

Instead of trying to hide the black feather by tucking it into her pocket or by tossing it aside, she stuck it back into her hair.

This was just the beginning.

Acknowledgments

I felt like Alice falling down the rabbit hole.

It began with a lot of phone calls and some super-secret negotiations. Before I knew it, I was sitting on a plane, heading for Los Angeles to meet with a bunch of executives at a toy company. I was a nervous wreck. What had I gotten myself into? So many people were involved in this project. Shannon Hale was writing the prequels. Why did they want me? Had this all been some sort of mistake?

The woman seated next to me was busy reading a script, ignoring my fidgeting. I couldn't focus on anything, my mind racing with self-doubt, so I glanced at her page. The watermark read: MATTEL.

"Um, excuse me," I said quietly. "I don't mean to be nosy, but do you work for Mattel?"

"Yes," she said. "I've been in Seattle on vacation. But it's time to get back."

"This is a weird coincidence," I told her, "but I have a meeting at Mattel later today."

"Really?" She smiled. "Wait a minute. I know who you are. You're Suzanne Selfors."

And so it was that serendipity had seated me right next to someone who knew all about my project and the world of Ever After High. And thanks to her warmth and good humor, when we landed two and a half hours later, I felt at ease. And that's how it's been ever since. Mattel has welcomed me, and even though they are the creators of this amazing, magical world, they've given me the freedom to dance around in it. And it's been a blast.

Thank you, Cathy Cline, for that plane ride. And to the creative team at Mattel—Cindy Ledermann, Lara Dalian, Julia Phelps, Christine Kim, Robert Rudman, Nicole Corse, Audu Paden, Venetia Davie, Ryan Ferguson, Charnita Belcher, and Sharon Woloszyk—much gratitude for all your help and support.

I've written many books with Little, Brown, but this time around, I got to work with a new enchanting editorial team. Thanks to Erin Stein, Mary-Kate Gaudet, and Rachel Poloski for helping this damsel de-stress.

Michael Bourret, you rule the kingdom!

Bob, you may not own a coat of armor, but I think you should be knighted. I became a writer because you gave me the gifts of time and love. Thank you.

And finally, Walker and Isabelle, you two are my Happily Ever Afters.

About the Author

Suzanne Selfors feels like a Royal on some days and a Rebel on others. She's written many books for kids, including the Smells Like Dog series and the Imaginary Veterinary series.

She has two charming children and lives in a magical island kingdom, where she hopes it is her destiny to write stories forever after.

Don't miss her next book, coming soon!

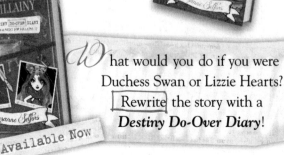

What would you do if you were Duchess Swan or Lizzie Hearts? Rewrite the story with a **Destiny Do-Over Diary!**

Available Now